# ESCAPE FROM...
# BOUDICA'S
# ARMY

**Andrea Pate**

## Dedications

To Carl for dragging me kicking and screaming over the finish line. To Phoenix and McKenzie, watching you grow up has been my absolute priveledge. The realisation that you will soon be starting your own lives has been the catalyst to restart mine.

And finally to Tracey, I am forever grateful for your warm support and English teacher's eye.

## Preface

These events took place in Camulodunum in the town now known as Colchester in Essex. While Ty, Addie and his family are fictional, the events around them are true.

ISBN: 978-1-9999691-9-6

First published in 2018 by Mckanix Publishing

This book is a work of historical fiction. Although the events described loosely follow real-life scenarios, the characters within this book are not representative of any person, alive or dead, and are purely fictional constructs.

# Contents

# Conquest
# 43AD

**V**assu sat perched in his hiding place inside the hollow tree. Growing right on the edge of the settlement, the ancient oak gave the safest vantage point from which to watch the surrender of his people. Filled with both fear and anger, he waited for the Roman leader to arrive at the tribal meeting. The Roman army had invaded the island of Britain a few months before and now they'd come to the great Trinovantes settlement of Camulos to accept the surrender of the local tribes and make their victory complete. Even at the young age of twelve, Vassu understood that his way of life would be changed forever.

Eleven tribes had worked together to fight against the Romans. Seeing these tribes work together was unusual but the threat from Rome was too great. If they wanted to win, they needed to put aside their differences and unite. Unfortunately, it hadn't worked. Despite their best efforts, the invading army managed to kill one of their most powerful kings and send the other into hiding. The Romans were unstoppable. Defeated, the tribal leaders agreed to meet the Romans here in the fortress of Camulos to discuss a truce.

All around them stood Roman troops, battle ready in case any of the local Britons decided to rise up against them. The army was unlike anything Vassu had ever seen before; hundreds of men stood proudly at attention.

Their form of dress looked strange to the young Briton. Instead of trousers, the men's legs were bare. They wore a sort of long shirt reaching to their knees with metal armour over the top. Vassu wondered how the men managed to keep their legs warm in this harsh climate. A few of the men wore strange metal helmets with what looked like a spiky horse's mane fanned out above their heads. They carried long rectangular shields, much bigger than the circular or oval ones that his own people carried. Some of the men held long poles with a golden eagle attached to the top.

The boy's eyes followed the long line of men as they spread out over the defensive earthworks south of the village.

His gaze stopped on something so strange that he had to shake his head to make sure he wasn't seeing things. The largest animals he had ever seen stood at the back of the soldiers. These grey giants had enormous ears and the longest nose he'd ever seen on any creature. The animal's flat feet could easily crush a man with one good stomp.

"Whoa!" he whispered to himself, "What are they?"

A soldier rode atop each animal like a horse, but it was clear that this was no horse. Whatever they were, they were terrifying.

As he watched what was going on around him, Vassu thought about the Roman leader they called Emperor Claudius. The boy had never seen an emperor before, but he'd heard enough gossip to guess that this must be the most powerful person in the world. Judging by how the Romans fought, the entire empire was indeed very strong. He watched as a grand chariot pulled by four powerful black horses appeared at the top of the hill. Unlike the small open-topped chariots used by his people, this one had four wheels, an arched roof and was large enough to hold several people. The vehicle rolled to a stop and a Roman officer rushed forward to open the door. Two well dressed men raced out of the carriage like bulls released from their pens. They were clearly grateful to be out. Before the boy could decide which one was Claudius, the men reached into the carriage and helped a third man down.

Vassu gasped when he saw a frail man stumble out. This man couldn't possibly be Emperor Claudius; there was nothing powerful about him yet, by the respect with which everyone treated him, it could be no one else. The Emperor's hands shook uncontrollably and his head bobbled on the top of his neck as though it would fall off at any moment. Claudius began to limp forward with the two other men standing guard on either side in case he stumbled.

Vassu couldn't help but giggle, "He's their emperor?" Vassu knew a man in another tribe whose body shook like Claudius's. With his disability, he would never have been allowed to lead any tribe of Britons. Vassu wondered how this man had become the Roman leader.

Vassu watched as Claudius was helped into the main roundhouse normally saved for large gatherings. The Roman generals and the leaders from eleven local tribes followed the emperor in; the great wooden doors firmly shut behind them. Inside those round walls, the fate of all the tribes of Briton would be decided.

The Romans had landed on the shores of this island several weeks before. This was not the first time they had come here. Many years ago, another emperor had twice arrived on the south coast. Both times the Britons had chased his army out. Most of the tribes thought the same thing would happen again. This time, however, the Romans had help from one disloyal Briton, Verica. He was the former king of the Atrebates tribe. The traitor had fled to Rome after he was cast out by his own people. With Verica as their ally, the Romans had new knowledge of this land and its tribes. This time, when the Romans arrived on shore they showed no signs of leaving.

The tribes gathered their troops for the coming battle and Vassu was happy to join them. With their two strongest kings, Caratacus and Togodumnus, they marched out to run the Roman invaders off their island. This time though, the Britons were defeated and the two kings fled with their armies.

Vassu hated running from the enemy. He thought it made his people look like cowards. "I knew we shouldn't have run away," thought Vassu and he was right. As the tribes ran, the invaders followed closely behind.

Twice, Caratacus and Togodumnus thought that they had escaped the Romans but both times they were wrong. The invaders were so eager to win that they even sent their men in full armour swimming across rivers. Vassu saw their daring crossings with his own eyes. They could not be stopped. After two major battles, King Togodumnus was dead and Caratacus was on the run.

The Romans sent for their emperor as soon as they were sure that they had beaten the Britons. When Claudius arrived, he helped capture Camulos, the tribes' most important settlement, and ended the fighting. The Romans ruled most of the land across the sea. It looked like, for Vassu and his people, their time had finally come.

# Friend and Foe
# 60AD

Sometimes the smallest choices in life can be the most important. For Ty, that choice was the simple act of going to school. He and his family had moved from Rome to Camulodunum a few weeks ago. He couldn't wait to make some new friends and get to know his new home.

In Rome, Ty had a tutor who came to the family's villa every day to teach him how to read, write and orate, the most important Roman skill of all. Ty liked to think of oration as learning to sound like you know what you're talking about, even when you don't. To his parents, a home tutor seemed like a good idea. After all, he wouldn't need to travel through the dangerous streets of Rome and he also had his teacher all to himself. The bad thing about having someone come to you every day was that you never got to leave your villa.

Having just moved to Camulodunum, he wanted to make friends. He begged his parents to let him go to the town school rather than have a tutor at home. There were only a few kids in this corner of the Roman Empire with parents wealthy enough to send their sons to school so Ty was hoping he could make friends with at least one of them. Since his dad was busy with his job on the town council and his mother was watching over the build of their new country villa, they didn't have the time to hunt for a new tutor.

That's why they agreed to let Ty attend the local school. Besides, Camulodunum was much safer than Rome. Their new home was in a quiet corner of the empire with very few people and even fewer ways to get into trouble. It was so safe that there weren't even protective walls around the town.

Ty's first day of school started out as any other. After waking up, he dressed in his favourite tunic and slipped his bulla necklace over his head. He ate a small breakfast made by one of the house slaves Viola, all the while dodging questions from his little sister Juno.

"Why can't I go to school with you?" she asked.

"Because girls aren't allowed to go to school," Ty replied.

"Is that because boys know girls are smarter than them so they have to study hard to keep up?" she asked with a playful grin on her face.

"No, it's because girls are so annoying we have to make up reasons to stay away from them!" answered Ty.

"OK, OK, that's enough," said Ty's mother Antonia. "Ty, get your things together, it's time to leave. Juno, you and I need to go to the new villa today. The builders said they're having problems with the hypocaust system. If they don't fix it, we won't have any heating and we'll freeze when we move in next winter."

"What?! But I don't want to go!" complained Juno.

As he listened to the two argue, Ty grabbed his stylus, wax tablet and the lunch Viola handed him. He squeezed all his things into a large bag and waved goodbye to his mother and sister before heading out of the door.

Camulodunum was built on the site of the old Trinovantes capital Camulos. It was also made the capital of the new Roman province of Britannia. It was the largest and most important town in the country. The Romans built it for retired Roman soldiers and their families. Unlike Rome, where the emperors were crazy and every few years an army would cross the alps to invade, Camulodunum was a very quiet and peaceful place to live.

School was a twenty minute walk from home. It was held in an empty stall in the forum between a couple of market shops. Ty made his way through the narrow streets of the town enjoying the freedom of his journey.

As he got closer to the forum entrance, he could hear the colourful noises of both traders and animals filling the square. Crossing through the archway into the large open courtyard, he took in the sights before him. This was one of the busiest spots in town. People from all over Britannia and the rest of the Empire came here to buy and sell their goods.

The forum was set out in a square with columns and shops lining three sides. A long building called a basilica made up the fourth side of the square. This was where Ty's dad Junius worked.

The shops lucky enough to have a spot beneath the forum's covered walkway were protected throughout the year from rain, snowfall and the rare hot day. The other stalls filled the forum square in a sea of canvas tents. In the middle of it all rose a marble statue of the winged goddess Victory, perched on top of a column proudly watching over the Romans as they took over a new land.

Throughout the forum, Britons, slaves and Roman citizens mixed together, discussing politics, arguing over prices, carrying goods and performing the tasks done every day across the whole of the Empire.

Ty passed by a stall which held large amphorae jars stacked on top of each other. He stopped to lean over one and was hit by the nutty smell of olive oil. Others, he guessed, held red wine or his favourite fish sauce. The slave girl standing next to him was arguing with the trader over the price of a small round amphora. Her accent was one he didn't know so he stayed to listen to her speak.

From somewhere deep in the crowd there came a loud bang and a scraping noise. People began flinging themselves in all directions.

Ty whipped his head around to see a loose donkey racing through the marketplace. It was dragging an upended cart, taking out everything in its path. There was no time to react, the animal and its cart were heading straight for him!

Out of the corner of his eye Ty saw a flash of colour. He hit the earth hard and his bag fell open spilling his lunch, stylus and wax tablet all over the ground. The donkey and cart flew past, continuing on its path, knocking things over as it went.

"Pay attention to what's going on around you!" shouted a voice in Ty's ear.

He turned to see a young boy with bright ginger hair and a sprinkle of freckles on his nose staring angrily down at him. He wore the strange leg coverings and checked pattern cloak of a native Briton, probably from the local Trinovantes tribe.

"Uh, yeah, sorry…" stammered Ty, although he didn't really know what he was sorry for.

Ty picked up his things and put them back in his bag before turning towards his rescuer. The boy was already walking back into the crowd.

"Thank you!" Ty called out, hoping the boy had heard him.

Without turning around, the ginger boy waved the back of his hand at Ty.

With one quick look at the mess left by the runaway donkey, Ty carried on to the other side of the forum heading towards his school. He was now running late.

A blue curtain acted as the school's door and Ty could hear a boy's voice coming through. He carefully pulled back the cloth and entered the schoolroom where a man with a white beard was sitting with two boys on wooden benches. They must be his tutor and classmates.

The man looked up at Ty, then asked the boy to stop speaking. Now all eyes were on the new kid.

"Are you Tiberius Junius Maximus?" asked the tutor as he rose from his chair.

"Yes, Sir," replied Ty respectfully.

"You are late!" shouted the man before he pulled out a long stick from the corner of the small room and asked Ty to place his hands on the seat of the chair. Ty was completely taken by surprise, it was only his first day and already he was getting caned. Ty did what he was told, then waited for his punishment. The other boys, still seated on their stools, quietly giggled.

Thwack! Thwack! Thwack! went the stick as it met with Ty's backside. With each painful swat of the cane, Ty swore to himself. He didn't dare let the words leave his lips in case it earned him another whack with the cane. "Now," said the man in a strangely calm voice, "that should teach you to never be late to my classroom again. Find a stool and sit down. I am your tutor Horace. This is Lucius and Cato. Lucius was just reading a poem by Ovid."

And with that, a red faced Ty placed his rather sore bottom on the stool and began his first day of school.

The rest of the day went by fairly quickly. When they were finished with the poetry, they moved on to writing lessons. Ty found that much of what they were learning he'd already covered with his tutor back in Rome. Horace seemed impressed by Ty's answers each time he was asked to speak. A few times he caught Lucius or Cato rolling their eyes at him which made him uneasy but there was very little he could do about it. Finally, Horace called time for lunch.

"I'm going out to stretch my legs. I'll be back in a few minutes. Finish your food before I get back." said Horace. Then he pulled back the curtain and walked out into the forum.

As soon as the curtain stopped fluttering, Ty felt something small hit the back of his head before bouncing onto the floor and rolling to a stop at the front of the classroom. The little pebble had been thrown by the smaller of the two boys, Cato.

"Hey, isn't your dad on the town council?" he asked.

"Yes." Ty managed to spit out around a mouthful of Viola's freshly baked bread.

"You must think you're special," replied Lucius with a sneer. Junius was in charge of collecting taxes and planning some of the town's new building work. Ty didn't know why Lucius would make such a big deal about his dad's job on the council, it wasn't like he was a senator.

Before Ty could respond, Lucius reached across with his long arms and snatched a chunk of meat from the bag of food Viola had made. Ty jumped from his seat to grab the meat back, but it was too late. With a nasty grin, Lucius popped it into his mouth.

"Mmm, this is tasty! Let's make a deal. Every day you're going to give me your lunch and, in return, I won't kill you."

"What? No!" cried Ty. Then, with a mighty shove, Lucius pushed Ty backwards causing him to trip over a stool and land on his sore bottom.

Just then Horace returned, "OK, I'm back boys. Let's get started." He peered down at Ty as he lay sprawled out on the floor. "Ty, I don't know what you're doing down there, but get up. It's time to restart our lessons."

Ty picked himself up and sat down on the stool he'd just fallen over. He kept quiet about what had happened between him and the other two boys. He didn't want to find out what sort of revenge they would take if he squealed on them.

When lessons ended Lucius and Cato raced out of the door. Ty neatly gathered his wax tablet and stylus, said goodbye to Horace and left the little schoolroom. Once he was out in the forum, Ty slowly made his way down the aisles between the market stalls. This time, he was careful to watch what was going on around him in case there were any more stray donkeys.

Near the exit, in the shadowy corner of the forum, Ty could just make out the shapes of three people in the throes of a fist fight. As he got closer, he saw that it was the two bullies from school, Lucius and Cato, fighting the ginger native boy who'd helped him earlier. The Briton hadn't been very polite, but he had saved Ty from an out of control donkey and cart. Lucius and Cato, on the other hand, had spent the day being horribly unkind. The fight really had nothing to do with him but Ty hated seeing innocent people being picked on.

Ty quickly made his decision and ran headlong into the scuffle, shoving Lucius with all his might. The taller boy was no match for the force of Ty's surprise attack and he flew into the nearby wall, hitting his face on the hard brick. Blood instantly began spurting from his nose causing Lucius to howl loudly.

Ty's charge had broken up the fight and distracted everyone enough so that the ginger haired boy could escape Cato's hold. He quickly gestured for Ty to follow and together they turned and ran back into the centre of the forum, winding through the market stalls.

Ty followed the boy through the maze of tents with Lucius and Cato chasing closely behind. After several minutes the boy in front ducked into a tent filled with bales of wool, brightly coloured woollen cloth and cheese. Ty dived in after him.

As Lucius and Cato approached, a large man with the same ginger hair as the younger boy stepped in front of the two bullies.

"Whoa, whoa, whoa!" he yelled. "Where do you think you're going?"

Fear shone in the faces of Lucius and Cato. "Nowhere, Bracius, Sir." answered Cato.

"That's right, you're not. Now get out of here!" Lucius looked like he wanted to argue but Bracius was a scary looking man. He tapped Cato on the shoulder and the two boys crept away.

Bracius looked over at his son Addie, taking in the boy's purple eye and swollen lip. "Those boys causing you trouble again, Addie?"

"Yes, Dad." he replied.

Bracius looked over at Ty, "Who's your friend?"

"This is…um?"

"Ty, Sir." replied Ty.

The man put his hand on Ty's shoulder, looked him straight in the eye and asked, "Is that boy's bloody nose anything to do with you?"

Ty swallowed before nodding his head.

The man's mouth twitched slightly into a smile. "Good. I can't stand those two boys. You can stay around here until I finish up, then I'll take you home."

Ty looked to Addie for permission. He wasn't sure that the other boy was completely happy with the idea. Addie had spoken very harsh words to Ty earlier that day and he didn't want to stay where he wasn't wanted. Addie looked unsure for a second then slowly nodded his head.

"You can stay." said Addie, "You don't seem to be like most other Romans."

Missing the point, Ty responded, "I am…I…I…I was born in the Roman capital! My dad is on the town council. I'm as Roman as anyone!"

"No, that's not what I meant. Calm down! Most Romans wouldn't have stopped to help me. They look at us Britons like we're…I don't know…not human, I guess."

Ty didn't know how to answer so he just said, "Well, those boys are bullies. They go to my school and they're not very nice to anyone. Besides, since you helped me earlier today, I guess I owed you."

This brought a smile to Addie's face. "Yeah, you did owe me!"

When Bracius had finished for the day, the two boys helped him place his wares into a small, tatty wagon hooked up to a pony. They headed out of the forum and on to Ty's house.

The two boys talked for most of the journey. It turned out that they had a lot in common. They had both just reached their 13th year and they both liked fishing and hunting. They had sisters but no brothers, although Addie once had an older brother who'd died of an illness several years ago. Both the boys' dads were important members of their communities. Ty's dad was a town councillor; Addie's dad was a descendant of the great Trinovantes kings and was seen as someone his tribesmen could go to for advice if they needed.

Soon they arrived at Ty's house. Instead of saying goodbye on the street, Addie's dad insisted on knocking at the door. Viola answered and when she saw who stood before her, she immediately called out for Junius.

To Ty's surprise, Junius and Bracius knew each other well. In fact, they spoke like good friends. Bracius explained what had happened in the forum between Ty, Addie and the two boys from school. Ty had been worried that his dad would be angry with him for getting into a fight but Bracius described it in such a way that Ty looked to be the hero of the story. In fact, Junius seemed proud of his son's quick thinking.

The topic changed to the townspeople and their poor relationship with the local Trinovantes tribe. As the two men spoke, Ty and Addie stood by their dads' sides listening in on the conversation. When the boredom became too much, the two boys began a staring contest, which turned into giggling, which turned into belly laughs. Junius and Bracius stopped their conversation and looked down at their sons.

"Well, I guess we should get going. It was nice seeing you again Junius," said Bracius.

The boys waved goodbye to each other and Ty watched as his new friend disappeared down the street.

The next day Lucius came to school with a red and swollen nose. He couldn't hide the rage on his face when saw Ty. As he made his way to his seat, he made a point of stopping in front of Ty, towering over him with a look of menace. Ty ducked his head and refused to make eye contact. Yesterday's bravery caused by a sudden burst of adrenaline had long since left him and now all he felt was fear.

"Is everything OK here boys?" asked Horace.

With one last glare at Ty, Lucius turned to Horace, "Yes Sir, everything is fine."

"What happened to your nose?" Horace continued.

"Nothing Sir, I tripped," replied Lucius.

Ty knew that the only reason Lucius would lie about his nose was to stop Horace from looking too closely at what was really going on between the two boys. This could only mean that something bad was coming later. Horace began the day's lessons and Ty tried to stop dwelling on his fears by concentrating on his work.

When lunchtime came, Horace gathered his things and headed for the door, leaving the boys on their own. Quickly, Ty jumped up and followed him.

"You're supposed to stay in the classroom Ty," said Horace.

"I know Sir, but I need to use the toilet," replied Ty. It was the quickest excuse he could come up with. He just didn't want to be alone in the same room as Lucius and Cato.

"Very well, but be quick about it," answered Horace.

Ty would have liked to spend the time wandering around the market. He could check in on Addie and see what he was up to. Unfortunately, the public toilets were next to the schoolroom and Horace was watching his every move.

When Ty stepped into the toilets, the smell hit him instantly. It was disgusting! A window was cut into the far wall, too high to see out of but large enough to help move the foul air around. It wasn't doing its job today.

The walls were lined with long benches with holes cut out of the seats. There were six holes per bench, twelve in total. Two of them were occupied. One man stood in a nearby corner hovering over a hole relieving himself. Another man sat toward the far wall actively contributing to the foul smell in the room. When he finished, he grabbed the nearest sponge on a stick and wiped his bottom.

Ty made his way to one of the empty holes. He hadn't intended to go but he didn't want to waste the opportunity. After he had finished, he stood in his spot as long as he could before he forced himself to make his way back to the classroom. His lunch break was far from over, but he couldn't risk angering Horace by spending much more time away.

When he got back, Horace was standing outside the classroom holding something in his hand.

"Eat with me today Ty, I'd like to get to know you better," he said as he handed Ty the packed lunch Viola had made for him that morning.

Ty gratefully took the food from his teacher. The pair began walking along the inner walls of the forum. Something about the look in the older man's eyes made Ty think that his reason for asking Ty to eat with him was untrue. However, he wasn't about to turn down the opportunity to avoid the bullies back in the classroom.

"Are you enjoying Camulodunum?" asked Horace.

"Yes Sir," replied Ty.

"When your dad has such an important job and most of the town know who he is, it can be difficult to fit in," continued Horace.

Ty was beginning to realise that Horace knew more than he let on. He didn't seem to miss much of what happened in or out of his classroom. Ty needed to answer very carefully; he didn't want to be a tattle-tale. He could admit that he wasn't fitting in but that might run the risk of exposing Lucius and Cato as bullies. This may help him for the moment but he knew that the two boys would retaliate if he snitched. His other choice was to deny that there was any issue. Ty did need help dealing with Lucius and Cato but not in this way.

In the end, he decided to steer the topic away from his classmates. "I met a boy yesterday who seems nice. He's one of the local Trinovantes people but our dads know each other well."

"A native?!" exclaimed Horace. "Oh come now Ty, I'm sure you can do better than that. Hmm, yes, you can definitely do better. Ask your dad to introduce you to someone more suitable. You don't want people thinking you can't make friends with real Romans, now do you?"

Ty didn't know what that meant exactly, but he was starting to understand that the native Britons were seen as second class citizens.

The two carried on walking for a few minutes until they were back at the schoolroom. "Now go inside. It's time to restart your lessons," instructed Horace.

Ty did what he was told and headed towards the classroom with Horace behind him muttering something about the lower classes knowing their place.

As soon as Ty walked into the room he could feel the glares from both Lucius and Cato. His trip to the toilets and his conversation with Horace only managed to put off any confrontation with the boys. They were still ready and waiting for a fight. Horace entered the classroom behind Ty, putting a stop to whatever the two bullies had been planning.

Over the next few days, school was a nightmare for Ty. As expected, Lucius and Cato took every opportunity to torment him. When Horace was out of the room or not looking, they took the opportunity to call him names, steal his food and throw things at him. They even managed to trip him over when he walked past their seats.

# The Bath House

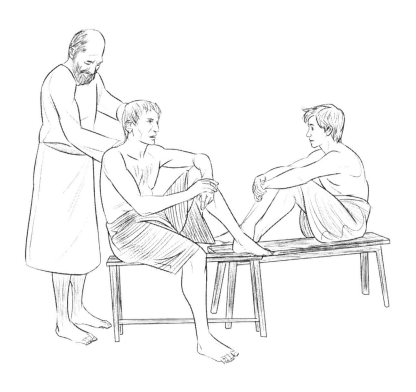

A public holiday meant that Ty had a couple of days off school. He needed the break from both the work and his two bullies. Junius and Ty decided to spend the first day at the bath house. Chrestus, one of the house slaves, went along with them to help. Junius visited the baths every day, but once a week Ty would come with him. This was a tradition that they had started when they lived in Rome.

When Ty and his dad arrived, they stripped off their clothes in the changing room and handed them to Chrestus. When they were completely naked, the pair headed into the gym.

Looking around, Ty could see other men playing ball games and lifting weights. Ty and Junius liked to use this room for wrestling. "I'm going to finally beat you today," Ty told his dad.

"Oh, are you?" asked Junius with a grin on his face.

"Just watch," answered Ty.

They began their match in the middle of the gymnasium, circling one another, looking for weaknesses. Ty moved first. Balancing on his toes, he hurled his body towards his dad, grabbed his arms and pushed forward with all his might. With a flick of the wrist, Junius freed himself from Ty's grip. Knocked off balance, Ty flew forwards. Before hitting the ground, Ty hooked his elbow into his dad's arm, swinging Junius around. They both lost their footing and fell onto the ground. Junius let out a surprised laugh at his son's swift movement.

Ty then reached around to pin Junius to the floor. If he did this right, he'd win his first wrestling match against his dad. At the last second, Junius broke free of Ty's hold and rolled out of the way. Ty quickly stood up ready for the next attack.

The pair carried on for several minutes, slipping, struggling and working up a sweat as they tried to pin each other down.

After a while they started to tire; one of them would have to make the final move soon. It turned out to be Junius. He reached out and grabbed Ty around the waist, trapping his arms to his sides. Junius lifted his son up into the air, swung Ty's legs to the side and then slammed him onto the ground. From this position, Junius was able to pin Ty down and win the match.

Out of breath, the two chuckled as Chrestus helped them off the floor. "Well done, Ty! You nearly had me there at the beginning", Junius praised.

Laughing and patting each other on the back, they moved on to the next room. This was the tepidarium. It was kept warm by fires lit under the hollow floor. The pair chose an empty spot on a long wooden seat to quietly relax and wind down from their wrestling match. Neither of them spoke as they sat next to each other watching other men come in and out of the room. After several minutes they moved on to the caldarium. It was so hot that Chrestus had to provide them with wooden shoes to protect their feet from the burning floor. The slave reached into a little pouch he'd brought from the villa and pulled out a set of bathing instruments. A flask filled with oil in one hand and a strigil in the other, he approached the father and son. Chrestus poured oil over Junius, making sure to slather it all over his entire body, and then did the same for Ty. When both Ty and Junius were oiled up, the slave took the strigil, shaped like a dull, curved knife, and began scraping the oil from their bodies. The little instrument removed any dirt, sweat and excess oil, leaving the pair fresh and clean. Afterwards, they found a spot in the steamy room to sit and allowed Chrestus to pour cool water over their backs.

"How are you feeling about our new home?" asked Junius.

"It's OK, I guess…," said Ty.

"It's not as exciting as Rome but your mother and I hope you're settling in. How's school going?"

"The other boys aren't very nice. I don't think they're very bright either. I like Addie, though."

"Who's Addie," asked Junius, then he remembered. "Wait, he's Bracius's son, right? They're a good family. Still, not all the Trinovantes are so nice, so be careful."

"What do you mean?"

"I mean, even though it seems like we're safe here in Camulodunum, we're surrounded by people who hate us Romans. It wasn't that long ago when we defeated their people in their own land. It may take a long time for them to forget."

Ty sat back and thought about what his dad had told him. He wondered how he'd feel if his people had been conquered and his way of life was changed so drastically.

The pair moved on to the final room, the frigidarium, which held a large swimming pool. Father and son settled in at the side of the pool to relax in the cool waters.

From across the room someone shouted Junius's name. He looked up and smiled as his friend Marcus made his way towards them.

The two men greeted each other and Marcus climbed into the pool, sinking down next to Junius. They spent a few minutes catching up on their families. Ty's ears perked up when they moved on to more important matters. He loved listening to his father talk about his work.

"So, have you heard what's going on with the Iceni?" asked Marcus.

"Didn't their Client King, Prasutagus, die a few months ago?"asked Junius.

"Yes, that's right," replied Marcus, "He and his wife Boudica wanted their daughters to inherit the Iceni lands and title. I don't know why he thought Emperor Nero would ever agree to women ruling. Of course, Nero being Nero, he put a stop to that," Marcus said.

"What do you mean?" asked Junius.

"Nero took back everything the Iceni owed the Empire; their money, goods and even their lands. He then had Boudica whipped to teach her a lesson. The two daughters didn't get off lightly either…"

Before he could finish, a loud shout came from the far side of the room. Lucius came running towards the water and with a great leap he hugged his knees and plunged into the pool. When he came up for air, Lucius found himself in trouble with the other bathers who had been splashed by his careless stunt.

Seeing his foe, Ty quickly scrambled out of the water and headed out of the baths. He didn't want Lucius to catch him here. He had made it back to the changing room and was halfway dressed when his dad found him.

"Is everything alright?" Junius asked.

"Yes, I was just ready to go," Ty replied. He didn't dare look his dad in the eye.

Ty wasn't sure if Junius believed him, but his dad didn't ask any more questions.

# The Coracle Ride

The next day, Ty made his way to the forum in search of Addie. He found him leaning against the archway at the entrance to the marketplace.

"Hey, I've been waiting for you," declared Addie, "Let's do something today."

"What did you have in mind?" asked Ty.

"I have a surprise for you," replied Addie. Curious, Ty allowed his friend to drag him towards Bracius's market stall. Once there, Addie told his dad that they would be out for a few hours.

"You boys be back by sundown," warned Bracius as he waved them off.

The boys headed through the maze of shops and customers and out of the forum. Ty followed his friend through the streets. With each new corner they turned, he wondered where they were headed. When they neared the temple precinct, he thought they might be going in to worship. It seemed like a strange choice.

With its white stone walls and high columns, the temple to Claudius was the grandest building in town. Ty peeked into the courtyard and watched as worshippers hurried to and from the temple, some with donations in their hands. They passed the temple and carried on up the street; it seemed that this was not where Addie was taking him.

The next place they approached was the amphitheatre. Ty thought that maybe they were going to see a play. Then he realised that it was too early for a show, so they couldn't be going there.

The boys carried on along the street, skirting the shops and houses until they reached the wharf. The docks were lined with boats being emptied and refilled with cargo. A strong smell of fish filled the air. Seabirds screamed from above as they eyed their prey and fought over food.

"We're here," said Addie.

"What are we here for?" asked Ty.

"See that man with the dark curly hair, the one with the limp? He's my dad's friend Otho; he has something for us."

Ty looked ahead to see a small man with a mangled leg helping a boat steer into port.

The boys wandered over to watch. They had to dodge the workers as they darted around the busy waterfront. This place was nearly as crowded as the forum. When they reached Otho, he briefly glanced at them then waved the boat into a free spot along the wharf.

"Good, you're here. You can help unload this boat once it docks," he ordered.

The boys looked out into the river and watched a large wooden boat slowly moving towards them. At the front of the ship stood a huge wooden goose's head, the symbol of the goddess Isis who looked out for sailors. Behind the goose's head stood a tall wooden platform which looked a bit like a small house. A man perched on top shouting orders to the crew below. The sailors listened closely as they pulled on the ropes and gathered the square sail to the top of the mast. Meanwhile, another sailor waited at the front with a long rope in his hand. When the ship came close enough, he threw the line towards Otho who reached out and caught it. The boys watched as Otho tied the boat down using a tricky knot.

After the ship was secured, the sailors quickly began unloading the cargo. Ty and Addie crossed the gang plank and followed the men down into the hold. Inside the belly of the ship sat dozens of amphorae. Some were short and fat, others were tall and lean. Like sleeping bodies, the tall amphorae rested against each other along the walls. Tied together with a long rope, they were secured in their place. In the centre of the hold, the fat bases of the short amphorae allowed them to sit safely on the ship's bottom without rolling or breaking.

The boys each leant over to grab a tall amphora. They were too long and heavy to carry in their arms so they hoisted them up onto one shoulder.

"What's inside these?" asked Addie.

"Fine wine in the tall ones, oil in the fat ones," replied one of the sailors.

They left the ship and followed the sailors along the docks and into a warehouse where they unloaded their heavy burden. It took nearly an hour for the cargo ship to be emptied.

"OK boys, I'm guessing you'll be wanting your payment. Follow me," said Otho.

Ty and Addie followed Otho as he limped his way to the back of the warehouse. In the corner under a large cloth sat what looked like a giant walnut shell. Otho grabbed the strange object and handed it to Addie. He placed it over his back, making him look like some sort of upright tortoise.

"You'll be needing this," said Otho as he handed Ty an oar.

"Come on then, Ty. Let's go."

"What are we doing?"

"We're going on a coracle ride. That's what this boat is called," said Addie, pointing to the shell on his back. "Not here though, this river is too busy. I know of a smaller one that runs past where I live."

"Where's that?" asked Ty.

"Near one of the old Trinovantes villages. It's an old hillfort south of the city. Most of us live here in town now but a few others still live outside town."

Ty wasn't allowed to leave Camulodunum without his parents. He would be grounded for the rest of his life if they found out he had been to one of the Trinovantes settlements. But he really wanted to try out the coracle so he kept his mouth shut and followed his friend.

"Why doesn't everyone live in the hillfort now?" asked Ty.

"It's not big enough to fit all of the Trinovantes. Our main settlement has always been here in the city. The Romans changed it into the city it is now. They made us do most of the work though. A couple of my uncles and some of my cousins helped build the temple. My family have always lived outside the main settlement. We have to live near fields to look after the animals, like our sheep."

The boys fell into an awkward silence. Ty knew that Addie was trying to put a good light on what had happened to his tribe. Even though he'd had nothing to do with Addie's tribe losing control of their home, Ty was still a Roman by birth. It was Ty's people who had conquered Addie's. For the first time in his life he was ashamed of the way the Romans treated other groups of people.

As they walked, the land went from wide open fields to a forested area. The plants became thick under the boys' feet. They had to duck under branches and step over high roots and plants. Despite the thick trees, Addie seemed to know where he was going.

Finally, the trees cleared and the boys came to the bank of a small river. Really, it was more of a wide brook. The water flowed peacefully along, taking the odd twig or leaf with it. Looking closer into the water, small fish could be seen flitting back and forth.

Addie removed the coracle from his back and gently placed it in the water. Keeping the boat steady with one hand, he lowered his bottom onto the narrow wooden seat. One at a time, he lifted his legs and placed them inside.

"Your turn. Just do what I did," instructed Addie.

Ty looked at the small space next to his friend. He wasn't sure they'd both fit in such a tiny vessel. Ty handed Addie the wooden oar then stepped into the coracle.

"Not like that…!" yelled Addie, but it was too late. The little boat teetered out of control. Ty lost his footing and fell backwards into the stream.

His head popped up out of the cool water, spluttering and coughing as he worked his way to dry land. Even through his wet hair, which was plastered to his ears, he could hear the squeals of laughter coming from Addie. Somehow, his friend had managed to stay inside the little boat.

"You're supposed to sit down before you put your feet inside, fool!" said a very unhelpful Addie.

A red faced Ty stood up and tried again. This time he very gently sat on the seat next to Addie before placing his feet in. The boat teetered slightly but stayed upright. Addie was still sniggering at his friend's blunder.

With mischief in his eyes, Ty leant towards Addie and placed his soaking wet arms around him in a great big bear hug. "Thanks for the help!" he said in the sweetest voice he could make, all the while drenching poor Addie.

"Ugh!" shouted Addie before both boys fell into fits of laughter.

After everything had calmed down, Addie grabbed the oar and placed its head into the water in front of the coracle. With the gentle swishing of a fish tail, he swept the oar under the water and the little boat propelled forward.

They sat in silence for a long time, happy in each other's company and the natural world around them.

They could hear the rustling of small creatures moving through the wood beyond the bank and dragonflies flittered around them. As quick as lightening, a bird with bright blue feathers and a brown breast dived head first into the water coming out with a small fish in its long beak.

"What kind of bird is that?" asked Ty, mesmerised by such an amazing animal.

"A kingfisher, you don't see them very often," replied Addie, his voice full of wonder.

This got the boys talking about other creatures found in the area. Addie told Ty about hedgehogs and badgers, which could sometimes be seen at night, and he pointed out the deer quietly lurking in the trees.

"We don't see animals like this in Rome. I think they live in the countryside, but you don't see them in the city," whispered Ty. He didn't want to disturb the deer as it nibbled on a thorny bush. Its head popped up every few seconds to peer at the boys as they drifted past.

"Well, what kind of animals can you find in Rome?" asked Addie.

Ty told him about the monkey his old friend Philo kept as a pet. He also talked about the time his dad took him to watch a gladiator fight. "Before the fight, there were some criminals put to death. They were sent in with a pack of hungry lions and the criminals had to fight them. Of course, the lions won. There was blood everywhere. It was so gross!" exclaimed Ty with a big grin on his face.

# The Trinovantes

The trees around them slowly turned to meadow and the stream made a sharp bend before it opened up onto a shallow beach. Rising up in the field just beyond the beach was a steep hill with a flat top. Sitting on top of the hill was a small village made up of about six roundhouses with pointy straw roofs.

Addie paddled the coracle over to the shallow beach. The boys climbed out of the coracle then pulled it onto dry land, out of reach of the running waters.

"Where are we?" asked Ty.

"This is where I live," answered Addie.

The boys climbed up the side of the hill and into the village.

"Our house is that one over there," Addie said, pointing to a building at the back, on the far right.

They walked to the house and stepped inside.

It took a second for Ty's eyes to adjust to the change in light. He was surprised to see that Addie's house was made up of one large circular room. The walls were painted with swirly patterns in black, yellow, blue and red.

A few simple wooden beds covered in furs sat against the wall on the right hand side of the door. Ty wondered where they went when they wanted to be alone.

57

An open fire burned in the middle of the hard dirt floor and a black cooking pot hung from an iron frame which sat over the fire. Steam spilled out of the pot, filling the room with the rich smell of whatever was cooking. Ty's eyes followed the steam up then stopped when he saw the leg of a wild boar hung up to dry along with different types of herbs. Ty's tummy began to growl.

On the far side of the door, an old woman squatted on the floor in front of a large loom weaving coloured strands of wool into a checked pattern. She stopped working and turned around to look towards the entrance where the boys stood.

"Addie!" she exclaimed, "What are you doing here? I didn't think you were coming home until after sundown."

"I've brought my friend Ty to meet you," he answered.

"Hello Miss," said Ty awkwardly.

"Well, hello to you!" she said as she rose from where she sat. "I'm Granny Cara," she said. "Have you boys eaten?" Before they could answer, she scooped something from the cooking pot and poured it into two wooden bowls.

Ty looked down at the steaming bowl of turnips and mushrooms in a broth. Taking the spoon from Granny Cara, he looked around for a place to eat his food. Unlike at his house, there wasn't a table or chair anywhere. Addie had sat on the floor in front of the fire, so Ty found a spot next to him.

The boys dug into their food. Mmm, it was really good. Ty could hear Addie slurping his food next to him. When they were both done, the boys stood up and handed their empty bowls back to Ty's grandma.

"Thanks, Granny Cara," Addie said through a mouthful of broth.

"Thank you, Granny Cara," repeated Ty.

"Your cousin Vassu is in the meeting house with someone, so try not to make too much of a nuisance of yourselves!" she warned as they headed back outside.

Ty had never been to a native village before, so Addie showed him around. Many of the buildings were for farming. There were homes for the animals, places to store tools, one for grain and another for food. What Ty had thought were six houses were actually five houses and one meeting house where the tribe gathered when there was something important to discuss. The meeting house was the largest building in the village. The entrance was supported by a tall wooden frame and two large wooden doors carved with swirly patterns. Above the door, attached to the straw roof, was the skull of what looked like a ram.

The boys remembered what Granny Cara had said about Vassu being in a meeting and quickly moved on. Addie was excited to show Ty the farm animals. He started by showing Ty the pigsty. The pigs had large pointy ears and bristly red hair that covered their plump bodies. They were happily lying in a large mud puddle in the middle of their pen. In the distance, black cows grazed in the fields.

Addie was most excited to show Ty the sheep. They were Addie's own animals and he took great pride in their care. Addie and his family raised sheep and sold the wool and cheese in the forum. Granny Cara made fabric which could be used to make clothes. They were really lucky because the Romans let them stay in their old village. Most of the Trinovantes were forced out of their homes and made to work for the Romans in town.

Addie's sheep had dark brown wool and curly horns. The cute, young lambs chased each other around while the older sheep grazed on the grass. One of the little ones had its head shoved under its mother's body slurping her milk, its little tail wagging with delight.

"I need to care for my sheep, want to help?" asked Addie.

"They don't just sit out in the field all day?" asked Ty.

Addie made a snorting sound with his nose, then in a playful voice replied, "No, City Boy, they don't."

The boys spent the next hour looking after Addie's sheep. They moved them from the large field into a smaller pen. They scattered what looked to Ty like weeds around their pen and plucked some of their wool, carefully placing the strands into a sack.

They were carrying buckets of water to the sheep pen when an egg came flying through the air, hitting Addie right on the forehead. Yellow ooze slowly dripped across Addie's eye then past his cheek before slipping onto the ground. Another one quickly followed, landing in the middle of his chest.

Ty and Addie looked around to see where the missiles were coming from. A girl who looked to be about eight years old peeked out from behind the granary. She had long red hair pulled tight into two pigtails and was wearing a yellow checked tunic that fell to just above her ankles. One hand covered her mouth as she tried to stop her high pitched giggling. The other hand held another egg.

"Evie!" yelled Addie as he dropped his bucket, scooped up a handful of mud from the nearby pigpen and took off in pursuit of the culprit. Without asking any questions, Ty scooped up his own clump of mud and joined the chase.

From the corner of his eye, Ty saw a flash of yellow dash behind the meeting house. He gestured for Addie to go around the left side while he sneaked around from the opposite side. They were going to cut her off from both directions.

As quietly as possible, Ty hugged the wall of the meeting house and tiptoed towards his target. When he found her, the young girl's back was against the wall of the building, her chest rising and falling as she caught her breath from the chase. Luckily for Ty, her head was turned as she looked in the opposite direction so she didn't notice him. He swiftly cocked his arm and let the clump of mud sail through the air. It caught her right on the back of her head! She turned around in surprise just as Addie appeared and hurled his muddy missile at her. With a loud thunk, it hit her on the shoulder.

The girl's face crumpled, "Not fair!" she yelled and then began to cry. Her little mouth opened wide with each howl and Ty could see the gap from her missing front tooth.

"You started it," insisted Addie.

"I'm telling Granny Cara!" she cried before running off.

"Was that your sister?" asked Ty.

"Yes, she's such a pain!" Addie said, annoyed.

With a great bang, the doors of the meeting house flew open and a large man with blonde hair and a ginger moustache came barging out, blue eyes blazing.

"You!" he bellowed as his eyes settled on Addie. "What do you think you're doing?! We're trying to have a meeting and you're out here making more noise than twenty cockerels at dawn!"

Addie looked down at his feet as he listened to the man scold him. "Sorry Vassu, we were just playing," replied Addie.

"You shouldn't be playing, Addie, you should be working. There's too much to do on the farm for you to be wasting time… and wasting eggs, I see," he added.

His eyes drifted over to Ty and widened in shock, a look of contempt sweeping over him. Vassu quickly tried to smooth his face but Ty could feel the hatred coming from the man.

In a voice as quiet and deadly as a snake, he said to Addie, "Get your Roman friend out of here, and don't bring him back."

Just then a woman stepped out of the meeting house. She was tall and beautiful with a pair of fiery eyes and a head full of long, curly red hair. She looked like a queen. Both the boys stopped their retreat to stare at the lady.

Vassu turned to her, "I'm sorry Boudica, I didn't know they were going to be here."

She looked down at the two troublemakers. Ty's knees started knocking together in fear. One corner of her mouth raised in a little grin; she knew the effect she had on people.

"It's alright, Vassu. They're just children playing children's games.

They're not yet old enough to know their place in this world. They'll learn soon enough, but not today," she said. Ty didn't know what she meant by those words, but he could tell that it wasn't good.

"Go on boys, do as you're told," she continued in a stern voice.

They nodded their heads at Vassu and the woman, both of them too afraid to argue.

When they were out of earshot, Ty whispered to Addie, "What's wrong with him?"

"That's just Vassu. His parents were killed when Claudius took Camulos. Vassu saw it all happen and my dad says he's been angry ever since.

They went back to Granny Cara's house to say goodbye to her and then walked down to the stream to collect their coracle and make their way back to town.

# Punishment

It took longer than expected to get back to Ty's house in Camulodunum. By the time they reached Ty's front door, the sun was already setting.

Ty pushed open the door and called out that he was back.

"They're home!" Junius shouted from deep within the house.

"Addie?!" followed the voice of Bracius.

The worried fathers appeared from around the corner where Junius's office was located. Both men were clearly very angry. Neither of the boys dared to move a muscle, they knew that they were in big trouble.

"You were meant to be home before sundown! Where have you been?" demanded Junius.

Even though the question was directed at Ty, Addie was the one who answered. "We took a coracle to Granny Cara's house."

"What?! You took him to the village?" asked an outraged Bracius. "You know he shouldn't be there!" he continued.

"I just wanted to show him…" began Addie.

"Don't give me any excuses. It's not safe for Ty to leave Camulodunum without an adult and it's definitely not safe for him to go to the village!" Bracius shouted.

He turned to Junius and said, "I'm so sorry. I didn't know that's what they were up to today. I'm taking Addie home now. I think it's best that they don't see each other for a while."

"But Dad…" argued Addie.

"Not another word!" ordered Bracius.

"I don't think it was all Addie's fault, Bracius. Ty knows he isn't allowed to leave town and he's supposed to be home before sundown," said Junius. "I think you're right. The boys need a break from each other. A week apart should do the trick," he continued.

Bracius nodded at Junius, "Yes, fine, a week. Again, I'm sorry."

The two men nodded to each other, then Addie and Bracius turned to leave.

"Bye Ty," Addie said in a voice filled with sadness. "Bye Addie," echoed Ty.

Junius closed the door and looked down at his son.

"I can't believe you left town. This isn't Rome, you don't know this place. Don't be fooled, Ty, the people outside Camulodunum are savages!" yelled Junius.

Ty was horrified. He was sure that his dad liked Addie and Bracius. How could he say such things about them? Ty's thoughts must have shown on his face because Junius' voice suddenly calmed. "Look Ty, I didn't mean that. I was just worried about you. This place isn't as safe as you might think. I need you to be more careful, OK?"

Ty looked at his dad from under his eyelashes. "Fine," he answered.

Just then, Antonia, Juno and Viola the house slave walked through the door. They had been to a party and were just returning home.

"Oh, look Juno, it's our two favourite boys welcoming us home. How lucky are we?" asked Antonia.

"Well, one of them is Ty so we're not that lucky," answered Juno.

"Brat!" came Ty's automatic response.

Antonia hung her cloak up, fluffed her hair and turned to get a better look at her husband and son.

"What's going on? Your faces both paint a picture." It was hard getting anything past Antonia.

"We need to have a word with you," said Junius.

"Ooh, what did Ty do now?!" asked Juno with a gleam of mischief in her eye. She loved it when her brother got into trouble.

"Juno, go to bed," demanded Antonia.

"But Mama…" Juno started to argue.

"Go! Viola, can you make sure Juno makes it to her room, please?" asked Antonia.

"Yes Mistress," she replied.

The house slave ushered a struggling Juno across the atrium towards her room.

"What's going on?" asked Antonia once Juno was out of earshot.

Junius told his wife what had happened. Like her husband, Antonia was horrified to learn that not only had Ty left Camulodunum on his own, but he'd also visited the old Trinovantes village.

"I think your dad is right, you need to stay away from Addie this week. I also think you need to pay a penance."

Antonia looked towards the ceiling as she thought up a suitable punishment. After a few seconds, Antonia's eyes came back to Ty's face, "Every day after school, I want you to go to the temple and make an offering. The gods need to know that you are sorry for disobeying us and for putting yourself at risk."

"What, that's it?" asked Ty, surprised at being let off so easily.

"Yes, but I get to choose the offering," continued Antonia. That did not sound good but there was no arguing with his mother, no matter how much he may have wanted to.

The next day on his way to school, Ty had to force himself not pass Addie's stall as he walked through the forum.

School was as terrible as it always was. This time, Lucius made farting noises every time Ty tried to answer a question. Cato struggled to control his giggling with each disgusting sound. It was so embarrassing!

Just before they stopped for lunch, Horace finally lost his temper.

"Enough! I've had it with you and your disgusting behaviour today Lucius. Go home! If you're not here to learn then go find something else to do."

"But… But my dad will kill me!" argued Lucius.

"He won't kill you, but he might give you a good hiding. Now get out," ordered Horace.

Ty and Cato watched in shocked silence as Lucius gathered his things and left the schoolroom.

"Are we ready to continue, boys?" Horace asked.

Neither boy dared argue, they just silently nodded their heads and got back to work.

As it turned out, without Lucius to start trouble, Cato was a much nicer person. He paid attention to Horace's lessons, answered questions correctly and never interrupted Ty when it was his turn to speak.

At lunch, the two boys actually spoke to each other in a friendly way. It started with Cato asking what Ty had brought for lunch. This led to Ty offering Cato a piece of the bread Viola had made fresh that morning. Then Cato offered Ty some fruit. Ty found the whole thing very strange, but he was glad for the peace.

When school finished, Ty gathered his things and left. He walked through the forum on his way to the temple precinct. Once again, he forced himself to take the long way around to avoid seeing Addie, Bracius or their stall. It was hard avoiding his friend.

Once he had made it to the temple precinct, Ty slipped through the archway and walked across the cobblestones. In the middle of the courtyard he passed the large bronze statue of Claudius wearing a toga. He held a small staff called a sceptre up in the air. In his other hand was a small plate held out, as if he were asking for an offering. A pigeon sat on the plate adding to the large pile of poo.

Claudius was the emperor who had conquered Britannia all those years ago. The Temple of Claudius was built in his honour using the taxes and workforce from the Trinovantes.

It was easily the largest building in the city, probably in the entire country. Made of white marble, it was surrounded on three side by columns with a red tiled roof. Wide steps led up to two grand wooden doors.

Only priests were allowed inside the temple but a special altar was set up just outside the doors. One of the priests stood at the altar reciting rituals for those wanting to make an offering or sacrifice. Ty climbed the steps and made his way to the altar.

It was only when Ty was standing in front of the altar that he got a good look at the priest. He had to do a double take because it was Vassu, Bracius's cousin! Instead of the long trousers that he had been wearing in Addie's village, he was wearing long white robes and a headpiece made from a thin metal chain that cut across his forehead. He may have been dressed differently to how he looked in the village, but it was definitely him.

It took Vassu a little longer to recognise Ty but when he did his mouth puckered like he'd been drinking vinegar. Vassu looked out into the crowds of waiting worshippers as if looking for a way to escape. He took a deep breath, cleared his face then looked back at Ty. Vassu stuck out his hand and asked Ty for an offering.

Ty reached into his bag and pulled out the pomegranate his mother had given him that morning. The red fruit was Ty's favourite, but they were expensive here in Britannia. This was the last one they had in their house. Since the fruit was at the end of its growing season, they wouldn't be getting any more for nearly a year. This is why Antonia suggested he use it as an offering. He was being forced to offer up the things he loved the most. His mother could be crafty when she wanted to be.

Vassu took his gift, recited some words and then tossed the pomegranate into the flame that flickered over the altar. Ty watched as the red skin turned black and crackled with the heat.

He was then told to say a prayer asking for forgiveness. He didn't know what to say. After all, he didn't feel any regret for going to the Trinovantes village with Addie. He was only sorry he'd been caught. Luckily, Vassu provided the words, impatience clear in his voice. Ty was asked to repeat them. When he finished the words, his first day of penance was over.

Ty couldn't wait to leave the angry glare of Vassu. He wondered how Addie's uncle had become a priest at the Temple of Claudius. It was a question he asked his dad later that night.

"I finished my first day of penance today," he told Junius when he walked through the door that evening.

"What did your mother give you as an offering?" he asked.

"Our last pomegranate," he sadly replied.

Junius chuckled, "Your mother is an evil genius. I learned long ago not to get on her bad side. Just wait to see what she forces you to offer up tomorrow."

Ty really wasn't looking forward to that. He didn't want to dwell on what else his mother would make him give up next.

Ty suddenly remembered why he'd come to speak to his dad. "I noticed something strange at the temple today. Some of the priests are native Britons." he said to Junius. Ty was smart enough not to tell his dad that he recognised Vassu from the Trinovantes village. No good would come of him reminding Junius of his bad deeds.

"Most of them are natives," replied Junius.

"What? How?" asked Ty.

"Well, when Claudius conquered this land, the native priests were called druids. They were smart, powerful and difficult to control so we had them killed. The Britons weren't too happy about it so we made some of them priests in our own temples and promised to pay them well if they did it," answered Junius.

Ty was surprised at the cleverness of the Romans. They had spotted that the Trinovantes would need a new religion to follow so they offered them the Roman gods to worship but let the locals lead the service.

The next day when he arrived at the temple, he checked to see if Vassu was there. A small line had already formed with a boy and two adults at the front. There was a different priest at the altar today. Ty wondered if this priest was also from the Trinovantes tribe. He took his place at the back and waited his turn.

Ty thought about what was in his bag today. Once again, his mother had chosen the offering. This time it was one of his old toys, a clay whistle shaped like a bird. When you blew into it, it made a little tweeting sound. Although he didn't play with it anymore, it had once been one of his favourites. Rather unkindly, Ty thought it was a good thing he didn't own any pets otherwise she might force him to make a blood sacrifice!

The family at the front had finally finished making their offering and turned to leave. Ty caught a glimpse of the boy as he passed, it was Cato. Their eyes met before Cato quickly hid his face in his mother's arm. He seemed embarrassed to be caught at the temple with his parents. Ty wondered why.

# Truce

Just as Antonia had instructed, Ty went to the temple all week. He saw Cato there every day too, although his parents didn't come with him. Cato tried to avoid Ty whenever they saw each other.

By the fifth day, Ty was tired of being ignored so he hid behind one of the fat temple columns and waited for his classmate. When he saw Cato heading down the steps, Ty rushed to meet him.

"Hey, what have you been doing here?" asked Ty.

Cato jumped a little in surprise. "Umm, I'm just here paying penance. What are you doing here?" he asked.

"I asked you first," Ty replied.

"I already answered," said Cato.

"No, you didn't," said Ty.

"Oh, fine," huffed Cato. "After Lucius was told to leave the other day, Horace came to my house to talk to my parents about the trouble I get into at school. My parents said I have to come here for a while or else I have to stop being friends with Lucius."

"Well, you should stop being friends with him anyway, he's horrible," said Ty.

"Thanks for your advice but I didn't ask. Now, why are you here?" asked Cato.

"I visited the Trinovantes settlement without my parents," answered Ty honestly.

"No, you didn't," replied Cato.

"I did!" Ty insisted.

"You're lying. Wanna know how I know? If you had gone to the Trinovantes settlement, they would have slit your throat. My dad says those people are animals. That's why we have to remind them who's boss. They can be like dogs who've forgotten their training," said Cato.

Ty was so disgusted by what Cato had just said that he didn't know how to reply.

"What are you talking about?" he said. "My best friend is Trinovantes and he's not a savage, he's great," answered Ty.

"I didn't say they were savages, I said they were like dogs. I mean, you'd think if you were really friends with one, you'd already know that. That's why I don't believe that you visited their village. Well, that and the fact that you're still alive. Anyway, I'm hungry. Want to get some food with me?"

Ty wasn't sure if a meal with Cato was such a good idea, but he didn't feel like going straight home. He agreed to go along.

The boys stopped at a food bar just outside the temple precinct to get something to eat.

"One sausage and bread, please," said Ty as he ordered his food.

"And I'll have the fish," Cato ordered. As soon as their food was served, they turned to leave, eating as they walked down that street.

They talked about school and their lives here in Camulodunum. They also talked about their families. Cato was the youngest of six. He had three brothers and two sisters. His sisters were both married, two of his brothers were in the army and the third lived in Rome.

Cato liked to play board games but rarely had anyone to play with, and he was really good with a slingshot.

"...I aimed my slingshot and knocked the head right off that squirrel. It fell out of the tree and its head rolled away," Cato told Ty. Ty didn't really believe Cato's story, but he was too nice to say anything.

As the pair talked, they tried to stay away from the topic of friends. Ty and Lucius didn't get along and Cato had already made it clear what he thought of Addie.

"Look," said Cato, "I know I give you a hard time at school sometimes."

"Only sometimes?" thought Ty but he kept that to himself.

"My parents told me I have to stop. I think Lucius is going to try to be nicer too," Cato continued.

"Uhh, OK." Ty didn't know what else to say.

"Yeah, so…I'm sorry, you know for…bullying you."

"Right, OK, thanks," answered Ty. "And I'll…try to be nicer too." He didn't really think he was ever anything other than nice, but he could see that Cato was making an effort so he did the same.

"Thanks," said Cato.

They came to a busy street corner and Cato suddenly stopped walking.

"Well, I live down here so I should get going," he said.

"OK, see you at school tomorrow," said Ty.

"Yeah, see you tomorrow," he answered.

Ty watched as Cato made his way down the street before he turned towards his own home.

He couldn't believe how well that had gone. He wondered if the truce between him and Cato, and maybe even Lucius, would last.

# Victory

Once Ty's week of penance was over, he was allowed to see Addie again. Of course, Ty's parents and Bracius made sure that the boys remembered not to leave Camulodunum again. To be fair, neither of them wanted to; their punishments had been harsh enough. While Ty had been giving away all his favourite things to the gods, Addie was given a new chore. As well as his usual duties of looking after the sheep, he was sent around all the other animals to collect their poo. It went into a large pit, then, when needed, the farmers spread the poo onto the fields to help the crops grow. Although it was a very important job, it was also really gross! Using a large wooden spade and a stiff brush, Addie would scoop up the smelly mess, dump it into a bucket and cart it across the village to the manure pit. It was the dirtiest, smelliest, most disgusting task in the village and for one whole week, it was Addie's punishment.

The forum was closed for the public holiday so Bracius walked Addie to Ty's house. The two boys were sent to the theatre while their dads discussed what they called 'Important Town Matters', whatever they were. Bracius warned them to be back as soon as the show had finished so everyone could get home on time.

They walked through the city to the busy theatre, passing the empty forum and the busy temple along the way. Once they got to the theatre, they looked around for a seat in the large outdoor space.

Rows of seats fanned out in a semicircle facing a wide stage. The further you were from the stage, the higher the seats climbed. Ty and Addie were lucky enough to find seats only a couple of rows back. They sat down and waited for the performance to begin.

A couple who looked to be about ten years older than the boys walked by them. When they saw Ty and Addie they stopped. "Hey, what do you think you're doing?!" asked the man angrily. The woman next to him clung to the man's arm and looked away in embarrassment.

Confused, Ty asked, "What do mean?"

"Not you! I'm talking to the scum sitting next to you. *Brittunculi* aren't allowed in the good seats. Go to the back like a good little doggie!"

Ty understood the word *Brittunculi* to mean 'nasty little Briton'. He couldn't believe these strangers could be so cruel to someone they didn't know. He turned to Addie who was busy staring into his lap, clearly uncomfortable.

"Come on Addie, we don't want to sit here, these seats stink of Romans," said Ty. The man looked like he might hit Ty, so the boys quickly got up and made their way to the back.

As they climbed the steps to the top, Addie whispered in Ty's ear, "Stink of Romans? What does that even mean? Besides, you're Roman too, you fool!"

"Well, I didn't know what to say. It just popped into my head!" Ty said defensively. Both boys burst into giggles.

They found a new spot along the top row and sat down. Their new seats ended up being much better. Even though they were further away from the stage, from their high spot they could see the entire city of Camulodunum. Rows of red roofed houses spread out around them. The countryside could be seen in the far distance. Just behind the theatre, the temple of Claudius towered over the other buildings and further beyond the temple was the outline of the forum.

"Hey, Ty!" came a voice from the crowd.

Looking around, Ty saw Cato making his way over to them.

"What are you doing here?" Cato asked in a friendly manner.

"We're collecting mistletoe," replied Addie in a voice dripping with sarcasm. Ty nudged his friend with his elbow.

"We're here to watch the play. There doesn't seem to be anything else to do around here today," explained Ty. "You can sit with us if you want."

Suddenly Addie started coughing and spluttering uncontrollably. Ty reached over and pounded his friend on the back.

"You OK?" asked Ty.

"Yes, sorry. I thought I heard you ask Cato to sit with us. It made me choke on my own spit!" whispered Addie.

"He's not so bad when Lucius isn't around," assured Ty, "Trust me." Addie didn't look like he believed him, but he didn't argue.

Ty turned to Cato and patted the seat next to him. Cato sat down and before the boys had much time to speak to each other the show started.

The play was called *Adelphi*. It was a comedy about a man who had two sons, one he raised himself on a farm and the other he gave to his brother to raise in the city. The city boy grows up to become wild while the country boy is raised to be a good citizen. However, things change for the country boy when he visits his brother in the city and meets a girl.

In the last act, the slave Syrus was given his freedom for the hard work he had done for his master's family.

The actor playing Demea, the father of the two brothers, gestured his arms towards the crowd and said in an artificially loud voice, "It is right he should be rewarded; other servants will be encouraged thereby…"

*CRASH!*

A loud noise echoed throughout the city. Ty, Addie and Cato jumped up from their seats and looked around. The sound had come from somewhere near the forum, but the boys couldn't see anything. A few screams could be heard coming from that direction.

The actors on the stage carried on with their performance but most of the audience had stopped paying attention. Panicked whispers spread throughout the theatre.

When no other noises could be heard, the whispers died down and the audience turned their attention back to the show.

When the play finished and the actors had taken their bows, people began to pile out of the theatre.

Sitting at the back meant that the boys had to wait until nearly everyone else had left their seats before they could make their way out onto the street.

"What do you think that noise was?" asked Cato.

"I don't know. I think it came from the forum. Let's go and check," suggested Ty.

The three boys hurried their way along the streets. The crowds were thick with people heading there too. When Ty and his friends got closer to the forum, they noticed people rushing around in all directions. Many women, and even a few men, were crying.

The boys passed under the archway and entered the forum complex, looking around. Because of the public holiday, the shops in the forum were closed and the area in the middle, usually filled with market tents, was mostly empty. A large crowd had gathered in there.

"I don't get it. What's wrong?" asked Addie.

He turned to look at Ty and Cato who had looks of shock on their faces. Their eyes were fixed on a point in the centre of the complex.

"What?!" demanded Addie.

"Look for what isn't there," said Ty helpfully.

As Addie searched the crowd again, his eye caught the column that stood tall in the middle of the complex. Following his gaze up he saw that the statue of the lady with wings which normally stood at the top was gone.

"Where did the statue go?" asked Addie

"It must have fallen over!" cried Ty.

"Ooh, I bet it's broken into a million pieces!" noted Addie, excitedly, "Shall we go and look?"

Cato turned to Addie, anger filling his eyes. "Look to see if it's been completely destroyed?! Are you insane, what's wrong with you? The goddess of Victory helped us defeat this awful island and your pathetic people. If she's fallen down that must mean something terrible is about to happen!" Cato screamed.

Ty could see that Addie was getting ready to hit Cato so he jumped between his two friends. "Hey, Cato, calm down! I'm sure it was just an accident," he said.

"This is an omen, Ty, I just know it. I need to go home. I'll see you around."

With that, Cato turned and ran out into the street, heading for home.

"Umm, I think we need to get back too. I should tell my family what happened," said Ty.

"Wait," said Addie, "I just need to do something."

He ran into the crowd while Ty stood on his own wondering what his friend was doing. A few minutes later, Addie emerged from the crowd with something in his hand.

"What do you have there?" asked Ty.

"It's a piece of marble from that statue. It broke off when it fell," Addie answered.

"Why would you take that?" asked a confused Ty.

"You never know when you might need something like this," said Addie.

Ty gave his friend a weird look, wondering what anyone could possibly need with a broken piece of marble. He was pretty sure that taking it was bad luck, but he knew Addie would ignore his warnings.

The two friends headed off to Ty's house. Addie noticed that his friend was being unusually quiet. He did his best to comfort Ty, "I'm sorry about your statue. I don't think it's an omen, sometimes things like this just happen."

"I hope you're right. That's not what's bothering me though. I can't understand why Cato has to be so awful to you. I don't like the way people treat you," Ty answered.

"Don't worry about it, I'm used to it. In fact, you're the only Roman who doesn't treat me that way. Well, you and your dad, anyway."

"Really? Why?" asked Ty.

"I don't know. They've always been like that. My dad says that it's been this way ever since Emperor Claudius came here. They forced most of us to leave our village and build this town, including the temple. Some of us were made into slaves and sent all around the

Empire. They even drove away our priests. We're supposed to worship your gods now but, to be honest, I'm not very good at it," said Addie with a wink and a grin at Ty.

They arrived at Ty's house and walked through the door. After a quick search, they found Antonia, Junius and Bracius sitting in the courtyard garden laughing together as they each enjoyed a glass of wine. Juno was sitting in the corner playing with one of her little wooden dolls.

Addie couldn't wait to tell his dad the news, "That big statue with wings next to the temple fell and broke today." Antonia gasped in shock, her hand flying to her throat.

"Really? That's strange. Did it do much damage?" asked Bracius.

"It shattered into millions of tiny pieces. People were running around screaming. It was ridiculous," answered Addie, matter of factly.

Bracius and Junius looked at each other and Bracius rolled his eyes.

"Oh, great! That's all we need right now, the townspeople losing their minds over an accident. I bet they're calling this some sort of bad omen," said Junius. Ty nodded and Junius put his head in his hands in despair.

Antonia was always the voice of reason. "Junius, you may think that a statue falling is meaningless but to most people in this town, a disaster like that is a real sign from the gods. There's already gossip amongst the slaves that the Iceni are trying to get the Trinovantes to join them in a revolt. It has everyone on edge, and now this. You have to do something to ease people's worries."

# The Druid

The next morning there came a knock at the front door. Ty left his bedroom and turned the corner just in time to see Chrestus, the house slave, opening the door. It was Addie and his dad.

"Is Junius here? I need to speak to him," a nervous Bracius said.

"I'll get him," said the slave.

"It's alright Chrestus, I'm here," Junius told him from behind Ty.

"Yes, Sir," answered Chrestus.

"Please, come in. Let's go into my study," Junius led his guests to the centre of the house.

Bracius got himself seated and the boys hovered nearby.

"I think something's coming, or someone, actually." said Bracius.

"What do you mean?" asked Junius.

"The other week, when the boys took the coracle to the village, my cousin Vassu was meeting with someone…" Bracius struggled to finish his sentence.

"Go on," encouraged Junius.

"Vassu wasn't meeting with just anyone, he was with the queen of the Iceni," said Bracius.

"Boudica?!" asked Junius, alarmed.

"She's trying to gather an army to attack the Romans," continued Bracius. "Look, I only found out this morning and I came straight here. I don't know anything else."

Junius stared down at his desk, his hands nervously hovered over the wood like he was trying to hold something important down.

"OK, I'm going to have to speak to someone about this. We need to prepare."

"Wait, I know someone who might be able to give us more information. I'd like to take you to him, but you'll have to promise not to tell anyone," said Bracius.

Junius wondered who this mysterious person could be. It wasn't like Bracius to be so secretive; this person must be very important indeed. He nodded his head in agreement.

Junius would have preferred to keep Ty at home but since Addie was coming along, he was worried that Ty might get himself into trouble if they left him out. Junius could keep a closer eye on him if they were all together and the two boys would keep each other company.

They left town through the western entrance, passing under Claudius's great marble arch. They walked along the narrow road for several minutes before heading off into open fields. The fields eventually turned into woodland and the ground became harder to walk through as their feet got caught in the undergrowth. All around them stood huge oak trees, each one more twisted than the next.

Finally, the trees thinned out and they came into a small clearing. In the middle of the grassy spot was the largest oak Ty had ever seen. The trunk was nearly as wide as some of the shops in the forum. Its long branches snaked out in all directions, many of them nearly touching the ground.

At the base of the trunk stood a man in long white robes. A hood covered his head making it difficult to see his face and his long grey beard stretched down nearly to his chest. He was busy stoking a small fire. A linen sack sat next to his feet, its top tied firmly shut.

"I've been expecting you," he said without looking up from his task.

Junius looked over at Bracius in shock, "Why did you bring us here? You know druids are illegal. Governor Suetonius is off with his army killing them as we speak!"

"Please, Junius. I know what this looks like but Duro is a friend. He wants to help so please listen to what he says," pleaded Bracius.

Junius turned to his friend in surprise. He couldn't understand why he would break the law in this way. It was very unlike him. He decided that it could only be for a good reason. Junius nodded his head to let Bracius know that he would at least listen to the druid.

Relieved, Bracius stepped forward, "Duro, this is Junius and Ty, the Romans I told you about. They've come to hear about your vision."

Duro turned toward Junius, his eyes staring straight into the Roman man's soul. After several seconds, the druid blinked and his eyes came back into focus. "You are known as a man who wants to do what is right for your people. I am here to help you choose the path you must take," he said.

Junius didn't know how the druid could help him but Duro was right, he only wanted to do what was right for the people of Camulodunum. People were upset since the fall of the statue of Victory. Rumours were flying all over town about how the statue had fallen. Whispers about a native uprising were getting louder. He decided to hear what the man had to say.

Duro asked everyone to sit in a circle around the fire. When all five of them were seated, he reached behind him and picked up the sack from the ground. The druid carefully laid a piece of cloth on the ground in front of him. He then opened the sack and pulled out a knife, a bowl, a small metal tool and what looked like a long stick. He carefully placed them on the cloth in front of him.

When he was finished, he turned to Bracius, "Do you have the item?"

Bracius reached into a little bag that hung from his belt and pulled out a small piece of marble. He passed it to Duro then sat back. Ty recognised the marble as the piece Addie had taken from the fallen statue of Victory.

Duro held the marble above the bowl then picked up the small metal tool. He used the tool to scrape against the stone causing flakes to fall into the bowl.

"Junius, give me your hand," ordered Duro once he was finished with the marble.

Junius leaned towards the druid and held out his hand, not sure of what was expected of him. Duro picked up the small knife and ran the sharp point across Junius's flesh. Blood welled up and began dripping into a bowl.

Duro picked up the stick and began to mix the blood with the marble dust. When he was finished, he slowly poured the mixture into the fire. The flame spat and danced, its colours changing into a fierce mixture of reds, orange, yellow and blue.

Duro stared into the flame for several minutes. The others watched the druid, waiting for him to speak. Finally, Druro blinked several times then looked around at Junius and the others.

"It's bad," he said. "The Red Queen seeks revenge. She will not be stopped. I see fear, death and fire. Can you hear the screams? You're all in danger," warned Duro.

"Who is the Red Queen?" asked Junius. "Tell us when this will happen!"

"It's not clear, but I think it will happen in a matter of weeks. You must leave here. Junius, you must get everyone out of the city before it's too late. Bracius, take them somewhere safe or they will all die!" The worry in the druid's voice was clear.

Ty and Addie's eyes were as round as a night owl's. The druid had frightened them with his talk of death and screams. Junius decided that he needed to get the boys back home.

"Thank you for your advice, Duro. I'll see what I can do. We must go now," said Junius.

"Wait!" warned Duro. "One more thing. This is for you alone Junius. Search for the ancient oak for it will save you."

Junius had no idea what Duro meant. He thanked the druid for his help then headed home.

As soon as the little group got back, Junius and Bracius went straight into the study. Ty and Addie tried to follow their dads but Junius stopped them.

"Go and find something else to do boys," he suggested.

They weren't about to leave without finding out what Junius and Bracius were talking about. The pair found a little hiding place next to the house shrine where they could listen in on the conversation without being seen.

"She's forming an army. You need to get ready to defend yourselves or get your people out of here!" Bracius's voice was filled with panic.

"We have no army! Like I told you in the forest, Suetonius has taken them to fight the druids on the Isle of Mona," answered Junius harshly.

The boys looked at each other, they had never heard their dads speak to each other this way.

"What are you talking about? Isn't this town made up of retired Roman military? Can't they do something?" asked Bracius.

"It's not that simple. These men are no longer fighting fit. Most of them are too old to fight Boudica's people. Besides, they have their families to consider. There are helpless women and children here," answered Junius.

"Our women fight alongside the men, Junius. For the sake of your people, you need to try to get them to do the same. Please Junius, this situation is more dangerous than you know," Bracius sounded deeply worried.

"I'll send for help. There has to be an army out there that isn't fighting with Suetonius. In the meantime, I'll speak to the council and see if there's anyone here in town who can help defend us," said Junius.

Just then Addie's arm knocked one of the little clay gods sitting in the house shrine. It wobbled then crashed to the floor, breaking in two.

"Ty! Addie! Is that you?" called out Junius.

"Uh, yes, it's us," answered Ty sheepishly.

The boys walked into the office, embarrassed that they had been caught eavesdropping.

"We should get going," said Bracius. "I'll let you know if I hear anything else."

When Bracius and Addie left, Junius sat down to write two letters. One went to Seutonius, the governor of Britannia, warning him of what was to come. He sent the other letter to Rome's special deputy here in Britannia. He asked the men for help defending Camulodunum in case Boudica attacked the town. He just hoped that they arrived in time.

# Banquet

It had been three weeks since Junius sent the letters and yet he still hadn't heard anything from Suetonius or Rome's deputy.

The townspeople were worried that something awful was about to happen. Rumours spread that the sounds of wailing could be heard in the amphitheatre and the basilica. Even as far away as Londinium, people were saying that the sea had turned the colour of blood and visions of a ghost town were seen in the river Tamesis. Fights between locals and Romans broke out all over the city.

Antonia decided to lift everyone's spirits by throwing a banquet. Together, she, Juno, Viola and Chrestus worked hard setting everything up. Invitations were sent, food was ordered and the musicians were booked. Antonia even had a special toga ordered for Ty. It was white with a red stripe along the bottom and reached to just below his knees.

Those on the guest list were mainly councillors and their wives. Junius planned to use the banquet as a chance to speak to the men about the real danger around them. He knew that not everyone believed that the natives were a threat. Some felt that if the Iceni did try to attack them, the Romans were strong enough to fight them off easily. Junius feared that if they did nothing to prepare, they could put everyone's lives at risk.

Antonia rarely invited children to her banquets but Ty was hoping that if Bracius was there, she might make an exception for Addie. As it turned out, Bracius wasn't invited either.

"Why won't Bracius be at our banquet?" asked Ty.

"Because I didn't invite him," answered Antonia.

"Why not? He and Addie are our friends," said Ty.

"Your dad needs the support of the councillors, Ty," said Antonia, "If a Briton shows up to eat alongside them, they wouldn't stay long enough to hear what your dad has to say."

"Couldn't Bracius help Dad tell people about what the druid said?"

"They wouldn't listen to Bracius, Ty, and you have to remember not to talk about that druid. Your dad could get into a lot of trouble if people knew there was one living around here and your dad didn't turn him in," warned Antonia.

"But he helped us! If they won't listen to Bracius and we're not allowed to tell them about the druid, how is Dad going to make them understand what kind of danger we're in?!" yelled Ty. With a small smile, Antonia looked down at her son and put her hand on his cheek, rubbing it with her thumb. "Relax, Ty. Most of the townspeople already believe something is coming. Your dad just needs to get the councillors to believe it too." With that, Antonia left the room leaving Ty hoping she was right.

The dining room was set for the guests to arrive. It was a grand room with a large mosaic floor decorated in a swirling pattern. The walls were painted to look like a beautiful garden with birds, flowers and even a little bird bath. A large square table sat in the middle of the floor. Three couches lined the table creating a U shape on three sides. The couches were close enough to the table so that the guests could reach the food while lying down. The family's best silver was put out, including spoons, bowls, plates and their special two-handled cups. The salads were already out, ready for the guests when they arrived.

Ty had calmed down a bit since he'd talked to his mother. He still wasn't happy that Addie wasn't invited but he knew Junius would try hard to get the town councillors to prepare for an invasion.

"The guests are arriving," announced Chrestus.

Antonia, Junius and the children took their places at the entrance to the dining room to greet their guests. Ty and Juno were only allowed to help greet the visitors. Once everyone arrived, Antonia ushered the children to their rooms and asked the guests to have a seat. The food was about to be served.

When Antonia returned to the dining room, Ty and Juno sneaked out of their rooms and found a quiet place to watch the party.

Each guest had their own sofa which fit around the table. They reclined on their left sides, talking amongst themselves while reaching across to the table for their favourite foods.

The first course was a selection of mushrooms, raw oysters, eggs in pine nut sauce and sardines. Every few minutes guests raised their wine glasses in the direction of a waiting slave who quickly ran over to refill their drinks.

The musicians stood in the corner of the room softly playing their instruments. One man strummed a lyre and another played the flute. A young woman sang along to the music.

Antonia was the perfect hostess; from her couch she was able to direct the slaves to bring out more food or fill a guest's cup. She was also very good at getting the councillors' wives to talk about things that were important to them.

"Martina, your armlets are lovely," Antonia said when she noticed the delicate loops of gold wrapped around the woman's upper arms.

"Thank you! They were a gift from my husband Felix. He had them made when he went to Rome last summer. He also had this ring made for me," said Martina as she wiggled her fingers in front of

Antonia's face. Martina's ring was gold with the shape of a dolphin stamped on top. "Oh, how sweet!" replied Antonia.

The second course was much larger than the first. Turtle dove boiled in its feathers, dormice stuffed with pork and pine kernels, pigs' udders and snails fattened on milk.

Throughout the meal Junius spoke to his guests about his fears. He told them how he believed the town was unsafe from attack. Since a wall would take too long to build, he suggested that they put up a fence to protect the people of Camulodunum.

"Now, Junius," said one man, "I think you've been spending too much time with that Trinovantes man. Can't you see that he's only telling you these things so you will fear him? Once you fear him, he has power over you."

Another man piped in, "You need to put that man in his place."

"A good beating would do him good!" said another.

They weren't listening. It didn't seem to matter what Junius said, none of the men at the banquet could see the danger they were in.

He decided to try using the fallen statue as a reason to protect the town.

"They still don't know what caused the Victory statue to fall. What if the gods were warning us about something?" asked Junius.

"Yes, they're warning us about the dangers of using cheap materials in our statues!" joked one man. The other guests roared with laughter.

Just as the party was tucking into the third course, dates stuffed with nuts, fig cake and apples in a cream sauce, a knock came to the main door. Junius and Antonia looked at each other in confusion, they weren't expecting any more guests tonight. Chrestus put down the jug he was using to mix water and wine and rushed out of the room to open the door. A moment later he returned with a high ranking soldier.

"Good evening," the man said to Junius, "Please accept my apologies for disturbing your banquet. I am Commander Longinus Sapeze of the First Hispanorum."

"Ooh, he's handsome," whispered Juno next to Ty.

"Shhh," said Ty as he tried to listen in on the conversation.

"Hispanorum?" ask Junius, "They sent me foot soldiers from a non-Roman unit? Did they send any horses with you? Or a real army?" Ty didn't know how his dad knew the Hispanorum weren't part of the main Roman army. From his hiding place he could see that his dad wasn't happy about it.

"No, Sir, the rest of the army is fighting on the island of Mona with Seutonius," replied the commander.

114

"How many men are with you?" Junius asked.

"Two hundred, Sir," he answered.

Ty could see a look of fear come across his dad's face. He'd never seen Junius afraid before and it scared him. If there weren't enough soldiers to protect Camulodunum, what were they going to do when Boudica and her army attacked?

"Your army has arrived, Junius," said Porcius, "You can relax now. We're all saved!" he said before bursting into laughter. His wife Fabia sat next to him looking very uncomfortable as she nervously fiddled with one of her gold earrings. "Porcius, please stop. What if Junius is right? What do we do?"

"Don't worry, my dear, these locals wouldn't dare rise up against the mighty Roman Empire. They lack the brains and the know-how."

Fabia didn't look convinced, "I'm not feeling well. I'd like to go home now, please," she replied.

"Yes, my darling. Junius, it's time we made our way home. You know how it is? If you're away too long, the slaves start stealing from you. Alright, well, good luck with your army but don't worry too much. These people aren't brave enough to go up against Rome. We beat them when Claudius conquered these lands all those years ago, and, if necessary, we can beat them again."

The banquet finished soon after Porcius and Fabia left. The mood had been broken by all the talk of the natives attacking.

# Escape Plans

**A** few days later things had calmed down in Ty's house. Although they were all still worried about what lay ahead, they were helpless to stop it. The family was sitting down for their evening meal, talking to each other about their day. Chrestus and Viola were busy placing the food on the table in front of them.

"Julia and I were playing knucklebones today and her brother kicked our pieces and scattered them all around the courtyard! Then he picked up the pieces that were left and ran off with them. And you know the worst part? I was winning!" complained Juno.

Antonia smiled down at her daughter. "Well, you'd better learn to like him. Your dad will be looking for a husband for you soon."

"Oh, yuck! Don't let it be him, Daddy, please!" begged Juno.

"We have time, Juno. Don't let your mother scare you. I'm not ready to let my little girl go yet," said Junius. He reached over and patted Juno's hand.

"Don't worry, Juno. You still need to learn how to look after a household before you take a husband. The way things are going, you may never get married," joked Ty.

"I'm going to kill you…" screamed Juno before launching herself across the table at her brother. A laughing Junius caught his daughter before she could do any harm.

"OK, OK, we've had our fun…" started Junius.

"Fun?!" shrieked Juno. She couldn't believe her dad saw her threats to kill her brother as fun. After all, she was being completely serious.

"Anyway," Junius was trying to ignore his daughter, "If this town is going to be attacked, we need to prepare. We need to put together a small bag with a few basic items in case we need to run."

"What sort of items?" asked Ty.

"Food, something to carry water, coins and perhaps a weapon of some sort. We don't know what we'll come up against," Junius said.

"Bracius has said that he will do his best to warn us before she comes. When that happens, we have to get out of the city as fast as possible. If he's not there to warn us then he'll try to meet us if he can," he continued.

"Why wouldn't he be able to meet us?" asked Antonia.

"Bracius has a cousin…" began Junius.

"Vassu," added Ty, helpfully.

"Yes, Vassu," continued Junius as he ruffled Ty's hair. "He's trying to force Bracius to join them in the fight. If he doesn't, Bracius is worried that he'll be called a traitor to his people."

"The tribes are so angry right now that they just might do something to hurt him and his family," Antonia added.

"Exactly," said Junius. "That's why we need to be prepared in case he doesn't show up."

"What are we going to do?" asked Ty.

"Like I said before, we need to get out of the city as fast as possible. We should head to Londinium. If Boudica's army can't be stopped then we can catch a boat and go back to Rome," said Junius.

"And leave Addie?!" asked an outraged Ty. "We can't leave him! No, I won't go!"

"Listen Ty, we don't want to leave but if the tribes of Britannia rise up against us, we might not have a choice. Hopefully, it won't come to that. I've sent another letter to Suetonius asking for his help. If his army gets here fast enough, they can stop her before it's too late," Junius said as he reached over and gave his son a soft squeeze of his shoulder.

The family spent the rest of the evening preparing small bags for each of them to carry if they had to leave quickly. Ty found it scary to think that they'd ever need to use it but his dad kept reminding him that it would only be used if the worst happened. Ty hoped that the extra troops that had arrived would keep any invader out, or at least give them time to escape.

# Invasion

**J**ust before dawn the next day, Ty was in bed asleep when he was suddenly awoken by a loud banging on the front door. Who would be here this early in the morning? Ty got out of bed and crept to the front of the house to see what was going on. Chrestus was already at the door; Ty's parents waited to see who could be knocking at this hour.

As soon as Chrestus opened the door, loud shouting filled the house. "Ty, Junius! She's coming, she's coming!" It was a very loud and panicky Addie.

"Boudica is on her way! Dad told me to get your family out before she gets here. He wants us to meet him on the other side of the forum," he continued.

All the yelling must have woken Juno too. She shuffled in rubbing her eyes and came to a stop next to Ty.

"What's going on?" she asked in her croaky morning voice.

"Go and get the bags we made up. I think it's time."

"What? Already?" she asked.

Ty didn't want to waste time answering his sister's questions. "Yes, now quickly, go!" he demanded shooing her towards the rooms.

Junius turned to Antonia and said, "I need to let the troops know. They have to be ready for her attack. Antonia, go with Addie. He'll take everyone to safety and I'll meet you when I can."

Chrestus quickly volunteered to come with him.

"There's no time to warn anyone! She'll be here any minute now," warned Addie.

"Junius, please, just come with us!" shouted a panicky Antonia.

Juno had just got back with the family's escape bags. Hearing Antonia's pleas, she cried out, "Daddy, no, come with us!"

"You know I can't. The townspeople need me too," he calmly told them. Junius cared deeply about the people of Camulodunum and wasn't going to abandon them in their time of need. He knew his family would be in good hands with Addie and Bracius. The rest of the people in town weren't so lucky.

Antonia, Juno and even Viola had tears streaming down their faces. Ty stood there in silence, shocked at what was happening around him.

Junius walked up to Ty and put his hand on his son's shoulder. "Ty, I need you to look after your mother and sister for me. I'll meet you as soon as I can but if anything happens, you need to take care of them."

Rather than let his dad know how upset he was, Ty placed his hand over his dad's and nodded his head. Junius squeezed Ty's shoulder then quickly turned to give Juno a hug and his wife a gentle kiss.

"Go! I'll be right behind you," he said to them, then he was out of the door, loyal Chrestus alongside him.

The family weren't dressed for the day but there was no time to change. They quickly slipped on their shoes before Antonia rushed them out of the door.

Boudica had chosen to attack the city just before dawn. It was light enough to see where she was going, but dark enough that her army could easily hide in the shadows. Addie's little group had the same advantages.

They skirted the western side of the city on their way to the forum. They kept their eyes on the fields beyond for signs of the approaching army. A loud battle cry filled the air and the little party froze in their place.

From over the crest of a hill, what appeared to be thousands of Iceni and Trinovantes appeared. Some of them arrived on foot, others rode in on chariots, some of them even brought fearsome looking dogs. Men and women alike marched forward, their faces painted with blue woad and their hair bleached white with chalk and sticking straight up off their heads. Most of them were dressed in traditional native clothing but Ty was shocked to see that some of them were completely naked. In their hands they held spears and shields, ready for battle.

In the middle of the crowd rode a woman in a chariot with wild red hair and fierce eyes. She held a long spear in one hand and the horses' reins in the other. She wore a brightly coloured cloak over her dress and a gold torc around her neck. Ty recognised her from the Trinovantes village; it was Boudica.

Junius must have reached the Roman troops just in time. Through the town's monumental arch, soldiers began spilling out of the city. They quickly lined up in battle formation ready to meet Boudica's army.

The Romans formed three lines. Ty recognised their tactic from stories one of his dad's friends had told him. Men on foot formed three sections, the left wing, the centre and the right wing. Soldiers on horseback moved to the far right of the troops to protect that side. Because the soldiers held their shields in their left hands and their swords in their right hands, their left sides were the weakest. The Roman troops tried to protect that side by standing next to some of the buildings that sat outside the edge of the city. There was little point, Boudica's army outnumbered the Romans nearly 500 to one.

As the armies faced each other, Boudica stepped off her chariot and faced her army. She shouted a few words to them, but she was too far away for Ty to hear her clearly. When she was finished, she reached into the folds of her cloak and drew out a hare. She held the small animal high above her head then gently placed it on the ground. The army watched as the hare scampered off into the undergrowth. Ty wasn't sure what that meant but her army seemed to think it was a good thing. They let out a loud cheer and some of them banged their spears against their shields.

Boudica climbed back onto her chariot, lifted her spear into the air and let out a loud battle cry. That was the signal her army were waiting for. They charged forward straight into the line of Roman troops. Despite having better equipment and training, the Roman numbers were just too small. They were soon hacked down by Boudica's angry army.

"Run!" screamed Addie.

Ty and his family didn't need any more warning, they turned and ran into the town, heading towards the forum.

The noise from outside the city was already waking people up. Bleary eyed, they stumbled from their houses to see what was going on.

"Boudica's here!" yelled Addie, Ty and his family.

This was all that was needed for people to start running.

"Get to the temple!" someone screamed.

"The temple walls will protect us," said another.

"Can we all fit inside?" asked someone else.

"Get out of the city!" yelled Ty, but he was ignored. The crowds forming on the streets were running for the safety of the temple. Ty hoped they were making the right decision.

Ty rounded a corner and crashed straight into someone. He was knocked back and nearly fell onto his bottom. A hand reached out to grab his arm and steady him. It was Cato. He stood there panting for breath with Lucius behind him. Their families were with them.

"You need to get out of the city! Boudica's going to destroy everything," warned Ty.

Lucius gave Ty a sneer, "We'll be just fine. We're going to the temple to wait for help. Once we're inside none of these savages will be able to get through the temple doors. We'll be safe there."

Ty could see that Cato wasn't so sure. "Please Cato," said Ty, "Come with us until it's all over." Cato looked over at his parents. His mother was crying, her head rested on his father's shoulder as he comforted her. Cato then turned to Lucius. The bigger boy's face was filled with his own self belief.

"You aren't actually thinking of going with him, are you?" asked Lucius.

Ty could see Cato was struggling to make the choice. Finally, his dad made it for him.

"Come along, boys. We don't have time to waste," he said.

"Good luck, Cato," said Ty, and really meant it.

"Yeah, you too," answered Cato.

The new friends waved each other off. Both of them hoped that they'd see each other again.

As soon as Ty started moving again, loud screaming was heard from the western side of town. Boudica's army must have got past the Roman troops. The escape party stopped running to look towards the sound.

At the top of the street, they could see the faint glow of a fiery torch charging towards them. As it got closer, they could see the shape of a woman on a horse and chariot. Her eyes were trained right on them. This was it, they had been caught! Boudica hoisted her long spear high into the air and screamed out another bloodcurdling battle cry. Behind her, the group could just about make out the shape of her army approaching.

She charged toward Ty and his family, her wild eyes trained on the group as they attempted to escape. The townspeople who stood between her and Ty were quickly cut down. Bodies went flying as Boudica's spear impaled them before tossing them to the side like the oyster shells at last week's banquet. Those lucky enough to escape her spear fell victim to her horse and chariot. It crushed anyone in its path. Ty and his family weren't going to make it; very soon they would all be dead, cut down by Boudica herself.

"Battle lines!" came a cry from one of the side streets.

Suddenly, there appeared a line of men standing in military formation between Ty's family and Boudica. They weren't members of the foot soldiers who had been battling Boudica earlier. They were part of the retired Roman military who lived in Camulodunum. These men were dressed in normal street clothes and they held whatever weapons they could find. Together, they were taking a stand against Boudica and her army.

Boudica quickly switched her focus to the troops directly in front of her. The men were clearly unprepared; she would be able to defeat them with ease.

"Run everyone! Go!" urged Antonia.

The retired soldiers could only slow Boudica down. Ty and his family needed that time to get as far away as possible. Addie, Ty and the rest of the group just hoped that they could get out of the city before she caught up with them.

When they reached the empty forum, they ducked through the arches to hide. Some of the people running for their lives followed them into the forum, but most carried on heading to the temple.

Ty and his family ran along the inside walls, passing all the stalls that were long shut for the night. If they stayed under the covered walkway, they could stay hidden in the dark for a bit longer.

Finally, they reached the far side of the forum and slipped back out onto the streets beyond; the sounds of battle still raging behind them. Screams from the townspeople filled the air as the Iceni and Trinovantes took their revenge on Camulodunum.

Once on the other side of the forum, they wound their way through more streets until they reached the eastern gates. It was fairly quiet here, so they were able to slip through with ease.

# Battle

They found Bracius waiting for them, standing under a tree with a large sack at his feet. Like the other tribesmen, he was dressed for battle wearing checked trousers but no shirt. His face and chest were painted with a blue swirly pattern. His hair had been bleached white and stuck straight up in the air due to the thick white limestone he had put in it. He carried a spear and a long oval shield.

"You made it!" he said, relieved to see Addie and the group.

"Where's Junius?" he asked.

"He and Chrestus went to warn everyone else in town," answered Ty.

The question on Bracius's face turned to worry. He looked up towards Camulodunum. "That sounds like him," he said.

"Here," he continued as he reached into the sack, "Put these on." He threw each of them a large piece of cloth which folded out into cloaks like the natives wore. They needed to look like Trinovantes, not Romans.

The group put their cloaks on then moved out towards the countryside.

Before they could reach the line of trees, a figure stepped out from the dark woods. It was Vassu.

"Hello Cousin. Where do you think you're going?" he asked.

Bracius stopped in his tracks and reached his arm out to the side to shield the rest of the group from Vassu.

Vassu was ready for battle just like Bracius. His body was covered in blue body paint and his hair was white like the other natives. The one difference was that Vassu was naked.

Ty had seen the other natives in Boudica's army fighting in the nude but now he was seeing it up close. It was so gross! He could understand why they did it. Fighting an enemy without any clothes on would distract anyone.

The sound of Bracius's voice brought Ty back to what was going on in front of him. "I'm getting these people out of here, Vassu."

Vassu screamed in response, "I don't think so! Ever since they landed on our shores, the Roman scum has made our lives a misery. None of them are leaving here alive."

"I'm sorry, Vassu, I can't let you do that. Junius has been good to us, you know that. He has tried to make our lives better. I know what they did to you was awful, but I can't let you murder Junius's family," replied Bracius in a calm voice.

"They're all the same, Bracius! We're all servants to our Roman masters. Every day I have to pretend to worship their gods. I have to say prayers for a man who stole the land from my people, a man who was made a god for his cruel acts against us. Claudius is dead. He isn't a god, he's a man who stole our lands and ruined our lives. All of his people should suffer as much as we have!" said Vassu.

With his speech over, Vassu lifted his spear and lunged towards Bracius. Bracius had just enough time to raise his shield before Vassu was on him.

Vassu's spear slammed into Bracius's shield with such force that his arm juddered. Staggering back, Bracius took a second to get a better grip on his own spear. He lunged at Vassu, leaping into the air and bringing his spear down onto Vassu's shoulders. At the last moment, Vassu raised his shield to protect himself.

Breaking apart, the pair then lunged at each other again. Both of them managed to strike blows on the other's shoulders and upper bodies. Vassu swept his spear low to the ground, catching Bracius's feet and causing him to lose his balance and fall to the floor. Vassu tried to drive his spear into Bracius's chest. Bracius quickly rolled out of the way and jumped back up onto his feet. As he straightened his body, Vassu came in for another attack. Quickly, Bracius raised his shield and smashed it into Vassu's face causing blood to spurt out of his mouth and nose.

Bracius rushed forwards. Vassu raised his arm towards him and their shields crashed into each other, making a loud cracking sound.

The fighting carried on like this for what felt like ages until Bracius dropped his shield, his arm aching from holding it in place for so long.

Bracius's breathing was heavy and his shoulders slumped forward, clearly very tired. Sensing the fight was nearly over, a little smile lifted the corner of Vassu's mouth. He let his shield fall to the ground and gripped his spear tightly.

Getting his second wind, Bracius held his spear in both hands and began using it like a staff against Vassu. The cracking of the wood as their spears made contact ripped through the air. Back and forth they went.

Vassu lunged his spear forward, the tip stabbing into Bracius's shoulder. He grunted in pain and blood trickled from the wound. He couldn't stop, though. This was life or death.

Ty watched the fight closely but he was also aware of the sounds of screaming that came from the city behind him. Death seemed to be all around them. Suddenly, Ty was back in Rome watching gladiators fighting to the death. Only this time, it was personal. This time, it mattered.

Vassu thrust his spear forward hoping to strike Bracius again. Seeing his chance, Bracius dodged the spear while at the same time reaching out for it with a strong grip. Once he had a firm hand on Vassu's spear, he twisted it around, moving behind his cousin. Bracius had Vassu's arm pinned against his back. If Bracius moved any further, he would break Vassu's arm. Instead of going in for the kill, Bracius grabbed his own spear and wrapped it around his cousin's throat. Vassu fought for breath, flailing around and smacking Bracius's arm in a bid to release himself from the hold. Bracius held fast, waiting for Vassu to pass out. When Vassu slumped forward, Bracius gently laid his cousin's body onto the ground.

The fight had taken most of Bracius's energy. Blood was streaming from his shoulder where he'd been hit. He managed to pick up his shield but he used his spear to help him balance on his feet.

He ordered the group to gather their things so they could get moving. The further away from Boudica's army, the safer they would be. Bracius gave one last look at his cousin lying on the ground, then he turned away.

A growling sound came suddenly from behind them. Bracius turned towards the noise just in time to see Vassu leaping towards him. As quickly as he could, Bracius pointed his spear in Vassu's direction.

The spear impaled him, going straight into his chest. Thick dark blood spewed from the wound. Vassu clutched the wound and made a gurgling sound before slumping over, dead.

Bracius stood over his dead cousin for several seconds. Pain could be seen clearly on his face. He never saw Vassu as his enemy; he only ever saw him as family. Antonia gently clutched his arm and pulled him away. They had to get out of there fast before someone else caught them slipping away.

The group ducked into the trees and made their way deep into the gloomy forest. They soon found the small river Ty and Addie had paddled down in the coracle. They followed it along for quite a while until they came upon Addie's village. Bracius pushed on up the hill towards the houses.

"We can't stop here, we'll be caught for sure!" worried Ty.

"We're not stopping. We need to grab a few things before we carry on. I don't know how long we'll need to hide. You wait here, and I'll be right back," said Bracius.

Addie, Ty and the rest sat down in the long grass by the stream. The sun could be seen rising over the hills. Ty wondered where his dad was and whether he had made it out of Camulodunum.

A few minutes later, Bracius came back down the hill with Druro the druid and Granny Cara.

Granny Cara and Evie met them at the bank with a small basket full of bread and cheese. They passed a piece to everyone. It had been hours since they had eaten and a lot had happened since then. They gobbled up their meal, grateful for Granny Cara's kind nature.

Bracius looked at Ty and his family. "Duro is going to take you from here," he said.

"Wait, we're not going with them?" asked a shocked Addie.

"If we're caught with them we'll be killed," explained Bracius. "We need to pretend that we're part of Boudica's army. That way we can get word to them if we hear anything new. There's a small Roman settlement west of here. Druro will take them there until they are safe to come back."

"No wait, we're supposed to go to Londinium! We planned it all out. Dad told us to go to Londinium. He'll be looking for us there," yelled Ty in a panic.

"Vassu said that when Boudica is done here, she'll be heading straight to Londinium. If you go there now, she'll catch up with you and you'll all die. For now, you need to go somewhere else." Bracius didn't mean to sound so harsh. He was just tired and worried about his friend. His job was to keep Junius's family safe and he would do whatever it took to get them away from Boudica.

"But Dad said…" started Ty before his voice broke and tears started dripping from his eyes.

"Hey, hey, hey, your dad won't be going to Londinium until after Boudica leaves. Why don't we do what Bracius says and go with Duro until she's gone? We'll meet Dad after this is all over, OK?" Antonia offered in a soothing voice as she rubbed her hand along her son's back.

Ty wiped his eyes and snotty nose on the sleeve of his cloak and nodded his head. Junius would never put his family in danger. If Boudica headed to Londinium after she was done here, he wouldn't want them going there too.

It took Ty and his family nearly a full day to reach the nearby settlement. They were taken in by a lovely family, a Roman man and his wife who was from the Catevellauni tribe. She was also Duro's sister. The couple had five children, all younger than Ty and Juno. The kind people took them into their home and gave them food, clothing and a place to sleep.

Antonia was very grateful; she spent her days helping out where she could. Sometimes she cooked meals, other times she mended clothes. Ty knew his mother was trying to keep busy as she waited for Junius.

News trickled in from people passing through. After the first day, they were told that nearly everyone had escaped into the temple. Ty already knew that from when they had fled the town. They were also told that those who hadn't managed to make it to the temple were captured by Boudica's army, tortured and killed. The next day they learned that the army had gone through every house, taking anything of value. They also pulled down the statue of Emperor Claudius which sat in the temple square.

On the third day, Bracius arrived with Addie. His face was the colour of chalk, his eyes rimmed in red.

"What is it?" demanded Antonia, "What's happened?"

"They've burned it," said Bracius in a croaky voice as though he'd been crying.

"What have they burned?" asked Antonia. She raised her hands to her ears as if she didn't want to hear the answer.

"The town! They put a torch to the temple last night with all those poor people still inside. As the temple burned, they started on the rest of the town. The whole of Camulodunum is in flames." Bracius's legs gave way from under him and he fell to the ground, crying into his hands.

Antonia let out a scream filled with more pain than Ty had ever known. The sound coming from his mother was like that of a dying animal. Both he and Juno burst into tears and ran to their mother. The three of them held each other as their grief took hold of them.

# Aftermath

Soon after setting fire to Camulodunum, the army moved on. They had destroyed the Roman capital, now they were headed south to Londinium. Once Boudica was out of the area, Bracius came back for Ty and his family.

Antonia didn't know where she would go now that they were on their own. Bracius offered to let them stay for as long as they needed; there was plenty of room where he lived.

Antonia was grateful for Bracius and Addie's kindness towards them. She knew that if it weren't for Bracius and Addie, they would all be dead. She also knew that whether or not the Roman army were able to defeat Boudica, she and her children were unsafe here without Junius. Once things calmed down a bit, she would have to make her way back to Rome. There her sisters could take them in.

Two days after Boudica's army left Camulodunum, Ty was helping Addie tend the sheep. When Boudica had passed through here, her army had stolen most of the animals. They needed them for food to keep them going on their march to Londinium. Granny Cara had acted quickly and hid some of them where she could.

Ty was counting the sheep in the field when he saw a man stagger out of the trees. He watched as the man made his way towards them. His clothes were in shreds and his face was black with soot.

He must have come from Camulodunum. About halfway between the line of trees and Addie's house, the man collapsed face first on the ground.

Ty was afraid to get too close in case he was dangerous. He waited a short time but when the man didn't move Ty knew he was either passed out or dead.

"Addie!" he yelled. If he was going to take a closer look, he wasn't going to do it alone.

Addie came out from the chicken sheds to see what Ty wanted.

"There's a man in the field. Come with me while I see if he's still alive," said Ty.

When they got to the man, neither boy wanted to touch him. If he was alive, he might try to harm them. If he was dead then they didn't want to touch a dead body.

Addie grabbed a stick and poked him in the ribs. After several tries, the boys heard a low moan.

"Flip him over," ordered Addie.

Ty bent down and gently placed his hands on the man's shoulder. With a big heave, Ty pushed him onto his back and got a good look at him.

"Dad!" yelled Ty. "It's my dad, he's alive!" Ty burst into tears and he wrapped his arms around Junius. Addie dropped the stick and ran towards his house calling for help.

Antonia, Bracius, Juno and Evie came running from one of the buildings. "He's alive! He's alive!" yelled Addie jumping up and down with joy.

When Bracius reached his friend, he bent down and scooped him up off the ground.

"Be careful," cried Antonia as she watched Bracius carry her husband to the roundhouse.

When they got inside, Bracius gently laid Junius on one of the beds. Granny Cara sprang into action, gathering herbs and other things she might need to heal Junius.

Antonia and Granny Cara worked all night tending to Junius's wounds. It wasn't until the next morning that he woke up.

Junius was hit with dozens of questions. They wanted to know what had happened to him, how he had escaped and what took him so long to reach them. Juno wanted to know if he'd saved one of her dolls.

Junius was too weak to answer all their questions but he told them that after he had warned the army that Boudica was outside the city, he and Chrestus started knocking on doors ordering people to run. They worked until Boudica's army reached them. Chrestus and Junius fought off a few men but Chrestus was badly hurt. When Junius tried to help his old friend escape from the city, someone sneaked up on them and stabbed Chrestus straight through his chest. Junius fell under the weight of Chrestus and hit his head on the ground and passed out. He didn't know how long he was out for, but when he woke up he realised he couldn't put any weight on his knee and when he tried to stand up he felt so dizzy it made him sick.

He crawled out of the city, passing out twice more before he found a hollowed out oak tree on the outskirts of town. He squeezed inside and from there watched as Boudica had his people put to death. When she set fire to Camulodunum, the flames were so strong the tree went up in flames too. He made his way into the forest before anyone could see him. When the army left, Junius spent the next couple of days trying to get to Bracius's home. He couldn't believe that he had survived Boudica's attack. It would take a while for him to heal from his wounds.

They spent the next few weeks listening out for news from Boudica's army. They learned that when she reached Londinium, she burned it to the ground just as she did at Camulodunum. The army then moved on to Verulamium and did it again. From there, Boudica headed north up Watling Street. She met Roman troops many times along the way, but each time she beat them.

It was somewhere in the centre of the country that Seutonius and his army caught up with Boudica. Met with the full force of the Roman army, Boudica lost the battle. Romans throughout the land could sleep soundly; their greatest threat had been stopped.

As for Ty and his family, Junius had written to Rome to let them know what had happened and asked for further orders. While they waited to hear where Rome would want them next, they happily stayed with Bracius, Addie, Evie and Granny Cara.

About a month after Boudica's army were defeated, Ty and Addie were sailing along the stream in Addie's coracle. They stopped when the ruins of Camulodunum came into view. The two boys couldn't believe the terrible thing that had happened to this great town.

"If it weren't for you, my family would be dead now," noted Ty, still a little in shock.

"Yeah, you would," teased Addie, then he gently cuffed Ty on the back of the head.

## The End

# The Real Story

The Romans invaded Britain in 43AD. Julius Caesar had been over twice before, but he never got very far. When Claudius became emperor, he wasn't well liked, probably because he may have had a disability like the one described at the beginning of the book. In order to stay in power, he needed people to like him. The best way for any emperor to gain the respect of his people was to conquer a new land. Claudius sent his troops to Britain. King Verica of the Atrebates had been kicked out of his tribe so he agreed to help the Romans. He gave them the information they needed to defeat the people of Britain. When the emperor's generals reached Camulos, they wrote and asked Claudius to join them. When he arrived, the Romans declared themselves the victors.

They built their capital city at Camulos and called in Camulodunum. The Romans forced the local Trinovantes out of their homes and put them to work building the temple to Claudius and other buildings in the town. The locals were forced to pay high taxes and were treated terribly by the Romans.

Some tribal leaders agreed to work with the Romans. They were called Client Kings and they ruled their people for Rome. The king of the Iceni tribe Prasutagus was a Client King. He was also Boudica's husband. When Prasutagus died, he left his lands and money to his two daughters. The new Emperor Nero wasn't happy with this deal so the Romans took back any land and money

Emperor Claudius had given them, they had Boudica beaten and her daughters attacked. Boudica was so angry that she vowed revenge.

Boudica asked the Trinovantes tribe next door to join her army. They had been treated badly by the Romans for years and agreed to help.

The Roman people of Camulodunum must have known she was coming because they called for help. They needed troops to help defend themselves against Boudica's army.

Governor Suetonius was away on the Isle of Mona, now known as Anglesey in Wales. He was there fighting the last remaining druids and he couldn't spare any troops. The man in charge of the country while Suetonius was off fighting was Catus Decianus. He was the one who gave the order to seize Boudica's lands and money. He sent only two hundred troops to help Camulodunum.

Before Boudica arrived, the statue of Victory fell down for no reason. The people of Camulodunum saw this as a bad omen. There were other rumours going around that the sea had turned red and dead bodies could be seen in the water, screams could be heard coming from the theatre and cries of barbarians were heard in the council chamber. The Roman people of Camulodunum were terrified.

Without help from the army, the town was helpless when Boudica arrived. Boudica's people killed everyone they reached. Those who couldn't escape locked themselves inside the temple. After three days of waiting, she burnt the city to the ground including the temple and everyone inside.

When she was done, her army headed to Londinium. Once there, they tortured and murdered everyone then set the town on fire. From there, she marched on to Verulamium and did the same thing.

By this time Governor Suetonius had heard what was happening and quickly moved his troops to meet Boudica. She marched her army north along Watling Street to meet Governor Suetonius. Unfortunately, her army was no match for the great Suetonius and the Romans won the battle.

We don't actually know what happened to Boudica. Some say she poisoned herself after her defeat, others say she fell sick and died. Whatever happened to her, Boudica will always be remembered as one of the fiercest enemies Rome had ever faced.

# Glossary

**Amphora** - Long thin pottery jars, often with a pointy base

**Amphitheatre** - An open air theatre

**Armlets** - Bracelets that go around the upper arms

**Basilica** - A long building used like council offices

**Bulla** - A round charm worn with a chain around a child's neck

**Caldarium** - A hot room in a Roman bath

**Camulodunum** - The Roman name for modern day Colchester in Essex

**Camulos** - The name of Camulodunum before the Romans took over Britannia

**Coracle** - A round boat shaped like a walnut shell or tortoise shell

**Frigidarium** - A cold room in a Roman bath

**Hypocaust System** - A type of underfloor heating used by the Romans

**Londinium** - The Roman name for modern day London

**Lyre** - A small musical instrument that looks like a U-shaped harp

**Roundhouse** - An ancient type of house with one room that is circular in shape

**Strigil -** A tool used to scrape off oil and dirt from the body, shaped like a curved knife

**Stylus -** A writing tool with a sharp point for scratching words on a wax tablet

**Suetonius -** The governor of Britannia during Boudica's uprising

**Tamesis -** The Roman name for modern day Thames river

**Tepidarium -** A warm room in a Roman bath

**Torc -** A thick circular necklace worn by ancient tribes

**Verulamium -** The Roman name for modern day St Albans

**Wax Tablet -** A wooden tablet covered in wax and used instead of paper, used with a stylus

## Follow in the Footsteps of Ty and Addie

To learn more about the Romans and native Britons, here are a few places you can visit:

### Colchester Castle, Colchester in Essex:

Built on the exact spot of the Temple of Claudius, the castle is now a museum. You can see a replica of the original temple and the Fenwick Hoard (a collection of jewellery like the kind Martina, a guest at the banquet, was wearing).

At special times, Colchester Castle allows visitors to explore the Roman Vaults. This underground structure was built by the Romans to keep the huge Temple of Claudius from sinking into the ground

### The British Museum, London:

The Roman Britain section of the British Museum houses lots of pieces from the time of the Romans including the copper head of a statue of either Emperor Claudius or Emperor Nero. The head was hacked off and found in a river years after the Romans left Britain. Be sure to say hello to Lindow Man. He is the mummy of a man who could have been one of Addie's family members!

**Butser Ancient Farm, Hampshire:**

Visit a village just like Addie's! You can even go inside the roundhouses to see how Addie's family really lived. While there, you can also explore a Roman villa.

**The Roman Baths, Bath:**

Find out exactly how the Romans bathed in one of the best preserved Roman baths in the world.

**Roman Amphitheatre, Chester:**

Explore the remains of a Roman open air theatre.

For fun and games and to learn more about this book go to

www.escapefrombooks.com

Printed in Great Britain
by Amazon

67831103R00097